Lisa,

Don't wait to be great!

The Briefcase of
Juris P. Prudence

D1531123

J.N. Childress

May 2016

This is a work of fiction. The names, characters, places, and incidents within are the product of the author's imagination or are used fictitiously, and any resemblance to actual persons, living or dead, business establishments, events, or location is entirely coincidental. The publisher does not have any control over and does not assume any responsibility for author or third-party websites or their content.

The Briefcase of Juris P. Prudence

To Josephine Crowell, my Granny, who always reminded me that I was her horse, even if I never won a race.

CHAPTER ONE

Staring at my bright pink backpack, bearing my name at the top, made me wonder if my parents knew that I would be a lawyer when they named me Juris Prudence. I often said my name out loud, just to think about the way it sounded when the name first came out of my Mom and Dad's mouths—Juris Providence Prudence. People usually had two reactions to my name—first, a strange look upon hearing it, and then the immediate follow-up question, "What does your name mean?" My immediate response was always, "It means the study of law."

"Green-line to Branch Avenue," the conductor shouted, interrupting my thoughts. I was on the metro, kind of like a train, but it only goes through the Washington, D.C. area. I've lived in Washington, D.C. my whole life, so taking the metro train was something I did often. My grandparents didn't drive, so we take the metro and the city bus everywhere. Actually, they took the metro everywhere; I preferred riding my bike around the city, but I was forced to take the metro if I couldn't ride my bike.

We don't have a school bus in Washington, so I have to ride my bike or take the Metro to get to school. I don't mind though. Getting to the National Kids Leaders Academy was always the most exciting part of my day. It was an adventure that was never the same. Whether I was watching the passengers on the train or seeing the sites of Washington on my bike, each trip to school was an adventure.

This was our first day back to school after fall break, but it didn't feel like fall at all. It had been snowing in the city for the past week, and the snow was up to our knees. Over the break, instead of raking leaves, we were building snowmen and sledding down hills. Snow was still piled high on the ground, so I had to wait until it melted to ride my bike again.

When I was on the metro, I would always try to guess who the different passengers were— where they were going, what they did, and whether any of them worked with the President. I always stood out from the other passengers on the metro train. They were all in suits and dresses, and I was usually wearing my uniform—dark blue jeans and a Kids Leaders Academy sweatshirt. On cold days like today, I would put on my KLA baseball cap to cover my long, black hair, which I usually wore in a ponytail.

"Gallery Place, Chinatown." This was my stop. I had to get off and transfer to the next train. My school was in Georgetown, and that was quite a hike from where I lived in the neighborhood known as Petworth in Washington D.C. I had about twenty-five more minutes on the train and then I would finally be at school.

A lot of my friends asked me how I managed not to get bored on the long metro ride to school. Between dreaming up stories about the people that I saw on the metro and reading the free newspapers that were given out every morning before I got on the metro, there was no way I could be bored on my metro rides. Sometimes, I wished I that could stay on the train and read and daydream forever.

Recently, the bad weather had caused me to ride the metro more often. During the past few weeks, my rides had been different than usual. Most mornings, passengers sat quietly and didn't speak to other passengers on the metro, but today, it sounded like a circus. It was the beginning of October, and everyone in my city was waiting on one big event, and it wasn't Halloween. It was the election of the next mayor of the city. Everywhere you looked, you saw gigantic red, white, and blue signs that read, "VOTE FOR SLY" or "GOODLITTLE FOR MAYOR." The election was the first week of November, and it had become the talk of the town.

This morning, I was reading a story about the two men running in this election— Sylvester Sullivan and Marty Goodlittle.

"Have you read what slimy Sly is trying to do?"

"Take away all healthy school lunches! Is he crazy?!"

"Kids don't need healthy lunches provided by schools! Their parents can send them to school with lunch. I don't care if it's healthy or not. I don't want my tax dollars going towards school lunches."

"Sylvester Sullivan has been a wonderful mayor for the past ten years. This city needs him."

"The new guy, Goodlittle, has one tough hill to climb if he thinks he'll win this election."

"I've heard some pretty awful things about Sly. Rumor has it that he has a criminal past."

This passenger's comment made the hair on my arms stand up straight.

I didn't understand what all of the chatter was about, and then I looked down at my newspaper that I had grabbed this morning. Now I understood. As I read the headline, I could feel my face heating up—I couldn't believe my eyes: "SLY VOWS TO TAKE AWAY HEALTHY SCHOOL LUNCHES. CHANGE WILL HURT NEEDY CHILDREN IN THE CITY," the newspaper headline read.

"Foggy Bottom, last stop in the District of Columbia." That was the cue that I had arrived at my stop. I didn't have time to be angry or nervous about the comment regarding Sly's criminal past. It was 7:45 a.m., and I had to be at school in fifteen minutes. I had no idea how I was going to make it to school in fifteen minutes with a foot of snow on the ground, but I had no choice if I didn't want to get a weeklong detention for being late to class. With my newspaper in my hand, I sprinted to the Kids Leaders Academy.

****

I arrived at the doorway of Ms. Nicholson's class at 7:58. I was out of breath, my feet were wet, and I realized that I had forgotten my lunch at home, but it didn't matter. I had two minutes before the clock struck 8:00, and I was on time. Last week, Ms. Nicholson told me that if I were late to her class one more time, I would get detention for a week.

Most students at KLA called Ms. Nicholson "Nitpick Nicholson." She would give you a detention for just about anything. Sneeze too loudly—detention. Talk without raising your hand—detention and clean off the whiteboard before leaving the classroom. Arrive late to class—detention for a week.

"You're cutting it close, Miss Prudence," Ms. Nicholson warned me as I limped to my seat.

I couldn't even say, "I know, Ms. Nicholson." I thought that if I said anything, I might just pass out because I didn't have any air left in my lungs.

The clock struck eight, and Ms. Nicholson wasted no time getting started. I was just hoping I could catch my breath before she called on me.

"Please get your homework out." Whenever Ms. Nicholson directed students to get their homework out, she scanned the room with her eyes, squinted, and pushed her large red-framed glasses up on her face. She was looking for anyone who did not have his or her homework.

I reached into my book bag, looking for the paper that I had stayed up until midnight writing the night before. I searched the front pocket of my bag. Nothing. I looked in the back pocket. Nothing. Oh-no. This was not good.

"Miss Prudence, is there a problem?" Ms. Nicholson hovered over me as I frantically searched for my research paper.

Yes, there was a problem! There was a major problem. I couldn't find my homework, I was still catching my breath, my feet were wet and cold from my journey to school, and my lunch was still on my kitchen counter. I couldn't tell Ms. Nicholson all of those things, or I would be guaranteed a detention for what she called being "discourteous." Ms. Nicholson was big on courtesy.

"No, Ms. Nicholson. Everything is fine, but I think I left my homework at home." I somberly replied. Everyone in my class was staring at me.

"Miss Prudence, late assignments are not accepted in my classroom."

"But, Ms. Nicholson, I have the assignment. I just need one more day to turn it in."

"One letter grade deducted, Miss Prudence."

"Not fair!" I realized what I had just said and immediately regretted it. One thing that I had learned during the last two months in Ms. Nicholson's class is that you never back-talked.

"What was that?"

"Nothing, Ms. Nicholson."

"Miss Prudence, you and I will be spending this week and next week together. Oh, and Miss Prudence, please don't forget to clean off the whiteboard before you leave class this morning."

Gosh! This was not good. Not good at all. "Spending time" with Ms. Nicholson meant good, quality detention time; detention time meant before school detention. Before school detention meant that I would have to wake up at 5:30 in the morning to make it to school by 7:00. If there was one thing in life that I absolutely detested, it was waking up early. I didn't even consider the fact that I would have to tell my grandparents that I had received another detention.

Detention with Ms. Nicholson would begin the next day, bright and early at 7:00 a.m. I couldn't concentrate during the rest of the class. Other thoughts were flooding my mind. *When will my socks dry off? How am I going to explain to Granny and Granddaddy that I got another detention? Will Sly Sullivan win the election and take away healthy lunches for kids? How on earth did I forget my homework? Did I do all that hard work just to get a B? What am I going to eat for lunch today?*

I tried my best to concentrate for the remainder of the class, but it was difficult. Ms. Nicholson's history class was my favorite class. Ms. Nicholson was a tough teacher, but she was a great historian. She had personal stories about every historical period that we studied.

Today, we were studying voting rights in the United States. I was an expert on this topic, and Ms. Nicholson would find this out tomorrow, once she read my awesome research paper.

"Does anyone know which historical women are famous for helping women to get the right to vote?"

I quickly raised my hand and shouted out the answer, "Susan B. Anthony!"

"Miss Prudence, please wait until you are called on to answer a question. Yes, you are right; Susan B. Anthony is one. Any others?"

I raised my hand again. This time, I waited for Ms. Nicholson to give me the green light to answer. Ms. Nicholson acknowledged my hand, and I quickly answered.

"Sojourner Truth!"

Ms. Nicholson nodded. "Very good, Miss Prudence. It looks like someone has been doing her homework."

I liked getting the right answers. This is why I always did my homework and studied before coming to class.

I have always been studious. When I was younger, everyone was amazed at how much I loved to read. When I was two years old, I wasn't reading kids' books; I was reading newspapers and history textbooks. By the age of four, I was writing long stories and reading them to my grandparents. My grandparents then decided to enroll me in the Kids Leaders Academy, a school for academically advanced children. I have been a student at KLA since I was five years old.

"Students, tonight please read chapters five and six of your textbooks. We will be discussing these chapters tomorrow."

As I wrote down my assignment, I thought about another assignment that I had for tonight, and that was to find out everything I could about the upcoming election.

CHAPTER TWO

When I arrived home, Granny greeted me with the best words that I had heard all day— "Honey, do you want some tea and cookies?"

"Yes!" I blurted with my teeth chattering. It was blistering cold outside. If I didn't feel some heat soon, I was going to freeze right there in front of my house.

I plopped down in my grandfather's favorite armchair. Granddaddy had the wood stove burning, and I was slowly beginning to thaw out. As I slowly ate the warm, sweet chocolate cookies that Granny had waiting on the stove, I tried to enjoy them, but I couldn't get Sylvester Sullivan out of my mind.

"What's wrong, honey?" Granny interrupted my thoughts. "Is your tea sweet enough? Are the cookies okay?"

"Oh Granny, everything is fine. I'm just— well. I'm just—oh nothing."

"Something's wrong, Juris. You know something? Those little almond eyes of yours get darker when something's troubling you. Tell me what's bothering you." Granny had a knack for two things. One—making the best cookies in the District of Columbia, and two—understanding when I just wasn't feeling my best.

"Granny, I'm nervous about the election. Sly Sullivan is the most evil, despicable human being to ever walk this earth. He wants to take away healthy lunches for kids, recess, and our school computers. He despises kids! We will have no rights at all if he's elected!"

Before coming home, I had spent a few hours researching Sly. My research confirmed what the passengers on the train had said earlier—Sly was out to ruin children. Granny poured some honey in my tea as I rambled on.

"I just can't stand the idea of seeing him as the mayor. It's not fair that kids have no say in this election. Why should it matter that I'm not eighteen? I should have the right to have a voice in this election. Sly shouldn't be able to rule me without my input!"

Granny just nodded. She never gave me an answer when I came to her confused. It was as if she knew that if I kept talking, I would come up with an answer myself.

"Granny, I'm going to do something. I'm not going to sit back and let him take away children's rights!"

My tea was getting cold, and Granny did not like when I didn't drink my tea while it was hot. She handed the warm mug to me, put her hand on my shoulder, and motioned me to drink. I took a sip, and before I could get down a full swallow, I blurted out, "I know what I'm going to do!" The tea exploded from my mouth, and I started choking.

"Oh my, Juris. Calm down, honey." Granny patted my back until I stopped coughing.

I caught my breath and continued, "I'm going to change the law, Granny!"

Granny never would tell me that my ideas were crazy, but I could always tell when Granny was skeptical. She nodded without saying anything.

"You're my horse, even if you never win a race." That was Granny's way of saying that she believed in me, and that was all that I needed.

****

It was 5:30 in the evening, and I knew that Sofie had piano lessons until 5:00 every Tuesday, but I was crossing my fingers and toes, hoping that she would be home and that she would pick up the phone when I called.

Two-zero-two-eight-eight-eight-four-five-five-one. I had dialed this number a thousand times. I could even say it backwards. One-five-five-four-eight-eight-eight-two-zero-two. Okay, no time for games—I had to run my idea by my best friend. The phone rang three times. As the fourth ring began, Sofie answered, and my heart slowed down.

"Sofie!"

"Hi…" Sofie always calmly lowered her voice when she could tell that I was about to erupt in a high-speed monologue about some new idea.

"Sofie, I know you're doing your homework and that you just got back from piano lessons, but I have to talk to you. Do you have five seconds? Okay, five minutes. I promise to keep it short." Sofie's parents were very strict about letting her talk on the phone on school nights, so I knew that I had to be quick.

"My parents aren't home. Señora Maria is here now, so I have a little time. My dad is going to want to check my algebra immediately when he gets home, so I can't talk long."

"Okay, well, you know how everyone at KLA is really scared about this election and Sylvester taking office? Well, I think there's something that we can do about this."

"What do you mean, 'something we can do'?"

"So, remember when we were learning about the Constitution during law school? Remember, that little rule that everyone is created equally? That means that everyone should be treated the same, including kids, right?"

"Yea…. I guess." Sofie sounded confused. I could tell that she had no idea what I was trying to say. I also knew that I had to make my point quickly. Sofie's parents would be home soon.

"Long story short, there's no reason why kids don't have the right to vote. Kids should be able to vote just like adults, and we need to make sure that happens."

"We?! You mean me and you?!" Sofie always stayed calm, so I could tell by the shock in her voice that she wasn't too eager to go along with this idea.

"Yes! You and me! Together, we can do this!" I tried to sound enthusiastic so that Sofie would believe me. "We graduated from law school, Sofie. We went to law school for five years so that we could use the law to help people. This is our chance to help people."

The Kids Leaders Academy had three different programs, one for medicine, one for education, and one for law. When my grandparents noticed that I was writing storybooks at just two years old, they decided to enroll me in the law program. They always knew that I was destined to become a lawyer. When kids are five years old, they were allowed to enroll in one of the three Kids Leaders programs.

The law program was law school for kids. We learned all of the stuff that adult law students learn, but we began learning how to be lawyers at five years old! By the time that we were ten, everyone in my law program had gone through five years of law school. When we turned ten years old, the KLA law students took tests that made us real lawyers.

Last year, I took an exam called the "bar" exam. After a lot of studying, I passed it, and now I am a real lawyer. Whenever I told people that I was a lawyer, they looked at me in disbelief. For one, I was still in school, and two, I was only eleven years old. I always explained to them that I had to continue going to school because I was not an adult yet, but that didn't mean that I was not a lawyer.

"J.P., this *sounds* like a good idea, but, I'm just not sure. I mean, it's not easy to change the law. Until 1971 when the Twenty-Sixth Amendment was passed, you had to be eighteen years old to vote. I just think it's an uphill battle to change the law."

My bubble burst faster than a balloon landing on a pile of needles.

"J.P., my parents are home. I have to talk to you tomorrow."

"Sofie," I sounded desperate. "Will you at least think about it?"

"I will. I promise." In the six years that I had known Sofie, she had never broken a promise to me. I knew she would think about this.

Unfortunately, her promise wasn't enough. I was terrified about Sylvester winning. I wasn't going to give up on the plan to get kids the right to vote.

CHAPTER THREE

My first day of detention with Ms. Nicholson was everything that I expected it to be—heinous. Not only was I upset about the fact that I had to serve a detention, but I was also horrified by the day's headline in the morning paper: "SLY CLOSES CHILDREN'S HOMELESS SHELTER. LEAVES HUNDREDS OF CHILDREN ON THE STREETS OF D.C."

Several weekends out of the year, my grandparents and I volunteered at homeless shelters for children in the city. Without these shelters, hundreds of children would have no place to sleep at night. Sly was out to destroy the happiness of children, and I couldn't let that happen. But for now, I had to get to detention on time, or I would have a whole different set of problems to worry about.

I arrived promptly at Ms. Nicholson's classroom at 7:00 AM.

I had only served one other detention with Ms. Nicholson this year. After that one, I vowed to never do anything to get myself into this position again. Yet, here I was, less than a month later, back in detention. During the last detention, I just sat at my desk for an hour, watching the clock as it slowly ticked its way to 8:00, the time that I would be free.

Today, Ms. Nicholson was sitting at her desk, working on her laptop. I was too afraid to ask what she was doing or to look at her computer, so I just kept my head looking straight ahead at the clock. It was so quiet that you could have heard a goldfish swimming in Ms. Nicholson's room.

"Miss Prudence," Ms. Nicholson began, "your paper on voting rights was quite good."

I was shocked that she was even speaking to me, let alone that she had complimented my work. "Thank you…," I hesitantly replied.

"You completed the law program at KLA." Ms. Nicholson asserted.

"Yes, ma'am, I did." I didn't know where she was going with this.

Ms. Nicholson didn't ask any more questions, and I had no idea why she asked whether I had completed the law program at KLA. She already knew that I was a lawyer.

The clock finally struck 8:00, and the bell rang. Thank goodness! I was free! I quickly got up and jetted to the door.

"Have a nice day, Miss Prudence."

I turned around, recognizing that I had been discourteous by not saying goodbye to Ms. Nicholson. "Have a nice day." I then ran out. I had to see Sofie before our next class started.

I ran down the hallway to Sofie's locker. I'd known Sofie since we were five years old. We began the law program at KLA together. She was also a lawyer. Even though I had talked to her every day for the past six years, I never ran out of things to talk to her about.

"Sofia Maria Flores-Ramirez!" I knew that calling out her full name would get her attention. I ran down the hallway and gave her a big hug.

"J.P., do you always have to make such a scene?" Sofie was very shy, and never showed too much excitement about anything. Her large blue eyes got bigger when she was excited, and her round cheeks turned slightly pink when she was embarrassed.

"Did you think about what I said last night?" I jumped right into what I wanted to ask.

Sofie was a thinker. She never jumped into making any decision, and I knew that this situation would be no different. In the KLA law program, Sofie graduated number one in our class. As our current class president, the whole school knew Sofie as someone who never made a quick decision. She always liked to get the right answer, not the quick answer.

"I did think about it."

"And?" I asked impatiently. My eyes pleaded with Sofie to tell me that she would help me change the law.

"Well, J.P., changing the law to give kids the right to vote isn't going to be easy. I mean, we do have to fight laws that have existed for hundreds of years."

"Well, if you believe that the Fourteenth Amendment is real, then you have to believe that all people are equal, including kids. Am I right?" I tried to persuade Sofie.

"I understand what you're saying, J.P. I just don't know that anyone else will buy the argument that kids should be able to vote. You have to be eighteen years old. That's the law. I know that Sly is terrible for children, but I don't know if that fact is going to change people's opinion that kids should be able to vote."

"We can't think about what other people will do. We have to think about what we can do. I know that we can get Sullivan out of this city." I realized that I was speaking loudly and that the students in the hallway were staring at me.

"That's right." Sofie was slowly beginning to change her mind. I could tell that when she started staring into space, the wheels in her mind were turning.

"Even though we are kids, we are lawyers. We have the knowledge to change things. If we don't use our knowledge of the law for good, then why do we have a law degree at all? Why do we have to wait until we are adults to create change?"

The first bell rung, telling us that we had five minutes until our next class started.

"Okay. I'm in. Let's do this."

I started jumping up and down. "Thank you so much, Sofie! This is going to be incredible! Just wait!"

Sofie nodded. I could tell that she was skeptical, but I knew that she wouldn't back out of this.

"What are our next steps?"

"Can you come to my house today after school?"

"We have a student council meeting today, but tomorrow should work. I have to ask my parents first though." I did not like waiting to get something started, but I knew I couldn't do this alone, and I had to wait for Sofie.

"Tomorrow it is. Let's get to class."

As I walked to class, Julian Cromwell, a student from the medical program, approached me. "You really shouldn't talk so loudly in the halls, J.P. You never know who's listening." Julian scolded. Julian was the biggest bully at KLA, always picking on students who he did not like. Everyone was afraid of him, except me.

"I'll remember that next time," I rolled my eyes and walked away. Nothing could dampen my mood. Sofie had given me her word that she would help me, and I was on cloud nine.

CHAPTER FOUR

Waiting for that day to arrive felt as though I was waiting for my twentieth birthday. I could barely sleep. Every hour, I would wake up thinking about something that I needed to tell Sofie—we had to let all of the kids in school know what we were doing; we had to figure out how the heck we were going to convince people that kids should be able to vote; and, we had to figure out who was going to help us do this.

In the middle of my zillionth thought, my alarm went off. It did not matter because I wasn't really sleeping anyways. Most mornings, I loathed getting out of my warm bed, but today I didn't mind. Getting through the school day just meant that I was closer to discussing my plan with Sofie.

Getting through the day was miserable. I have no clue what any of my teachers said during class. Making sure that Sylvester Sullivan did not get elected was my top priority.

During my history class, Ms. Nicholson could sense that I was preoccupied.

"Miss Prudence, the whiteboard is in front of you, not on the ceiling." I quickly redirected my eyes and my head to face forward, instead of the ceiling. Daydreaming about how I would get kids the right to vote had put my mind in the clouds.

I slugged through the day, and finally, it ended. My notepad had ten pages filled with notes about how we would change the law.

****

I jolted home on my bike immediately after school ended. I didn't want to talk to anyone, unless it was Sofie. When I got in the house, Granny greeted me with her usual, "Hello, honey. How was your day? I made some peanut brittle, do you want any?"

I loved Granny's peanut brittle more than anything. The sugar, caramel, and peanut combination seemed to melt in my mouth. While I usually never rejected peanut brittle, the one thing that I wanted more than anything at that moment was to talk to Sofie. "No thanks, Granny. Has Sofie called?"

Granny did not like when someone did not want her food, and her face showed it. "You don't want my peanut brittle?" Granny totally ignored the question that I'd asked about Sofie.

"Sure, Granny." I could not hide my preoccupation. "I don't want too much—"

Before I could finish, the phone rang. Granny walked to catch it, but I sprinted towards it, reaching it before her.

"Hello?!" I shouted, hoping desperately that Sofie was on the other end of the line.

"Hi... JP..." Sofie responded apprehensively. She knew that I was getting impatient.

"Where are you?! I thought we were meeting at three this afternoon."

"Calm down. I'm on my way. My driver was running late."

Sofie had a personal driver to pick her up from her after school activities. Today, she was coming from her student council meeting.

"Okay. Great. Can't wait until you get here. We have a bunch to talk about. Oh, by the way, Granny made your favorite—peanut brittle."

"Yippeeeee! Be there soon."

I hung up the phone and paced back and forth, looking out of the window for Sofie's black car to pull up. It seemed like one hundred years before Sofie arrived, but finally, she was there.

"Sofie!" I shouted, as I opened the door.

"Hi, J.P.…. Can I get some peanut brittle?" Sofie was focused on peanut brittle, but I wanted to discuss business.

"Sofie! Hello, honey!" Granny exclaimed from the kitchen. "I made this just for you." Granny walked out with a slice of peanut brittle the size of the entire plate. "I cut you a big piece so that you can take some home."

"Thanks so much, Granny!" Sofie hugged Granny as if Granny had just given her a million dollars.

"You can bring that downstairs, Sofie. We don't have much time, and we have a lot to do." Sofie had to be home by 5:00, and it was already almost 4:00. We had little more than a half hour before Sofie would have to leave in order to make it home in time.

We walked downstairs to the basement. Granny and Granddaddy had set up an office in the basement where I did my homework each day. This was also the part of my house where I spent my quiet time reading. Granddaddy had built me my own desk and two small chairs. Sofie sat down, and I remained standing by my chalkboard that Granddaddy recently bought me. I usually used this board to write down all of my homework assignments, but today it had a new purpose—to map out my plan of how we were going to make sure that Sylvester did not win this election.

"Let's get started," I stated confidently.

Sofie listened attentively. I knew that I had captured her interest. "Sylvester has been in office for ten years. Since then, he has closed homeless shelters for kids and vowed to take away healthy school lunches for kids. Even worse, reports have come out that he has a criminal past, involving crimes against children." Sofie continued to listen attentively. I wrote out the facts that I had just mentioned on my chalkboard.

"So, how are we going to get Sly out of office, J.P.?" Sofie asked.

"We need to use our knowledge of the law to change the law. If we can get kids the right to vote, Sylvester will lose this election."

"When you say 'kids,' do you mean all kids, or just kids over a certain age? I mean, we can't expect three-year-olds to vote."

"I think that at the age of seven, kids are smart enough to make their own decisions, so I think that all kids who are seven years old and older should be able to vote," I responded to

Sofie's question. I wrote down the words, "law" and "7 years old" on my chalkboard.

"Sylvester's opponent, Marty Goodlittle, has been supporting children for years. He helped to open a children's hospital a year ago." I wrote down the words, "Marty Goodlittle" and "children's hospital" on my chalkboard. "Marty has donated millions of dollars to kids' charities. He has promised to make sure that all schools have healthy lunches. On the news, he said that he vows to make sure that kids are given great teachers in all schools in our city. We have to get Marty in office, and getting kids the right to vote is how we are going to do it."

"I'm listening...," Sofie stated, interested in what I was about to say.

"You're my best friend and the smartest person I know. First, I need to know that you're in. I need to know that you can give me your full support to help make this happen."

"J.P, you're my best friend, too, and you know that I will do anything I can to support you. This is important. I mean, it will be absolutely huge if we can get this done. I'm in." I could tell that Sofie was excited about our new project.

"Great!" I breathed a sigh of relief. However, I knew we were running out of time, and I didn't have time to celebrate too much. I had to finish discussing everything before Sofie had to leave. "Second, we need help if we are going to get this done."

"Who do you think will help us?" Sofie asked.

"Well, I've been thinking. Who are our best friends? Who has never let us down? Who went through five hard years of law school with us?" I could already tell that Sofie knew that I wanted our two other best friends, who were also lawyers, to join our team.

"Izzy and Maddy," Sofie answered immediately, interrupting my memories about my law school days.

"Absolutely! I want them on our team. With them, we will be unstoppable."

"Okay, let's get to it. Let's call them and see if they will come on board."

Without taking a breath, I called Maddy. "Hi, is Maddy available?"

"Yes, hold on one second," I heard Mr. Rosenfeld say.

"Madeline, telephone. Don't stay on too long. We are having dinner soon."

"Hello?" Maddy answered in her usual high-pitched voice, overflowing with enthusiasm.

"Hi, Maddy. It's J.P."

"Howdy, J.P. Whatcha' up to?"

"Sofie and I are discussing some serious business that we'd like you to help us with. Can you meet us at my house on...?" Covering the phone with my hand, I whispered to Sofia, "Can you come back to my house on Friday after school?" Sofie nodded yes. "Maddy, can you come over after school on Friday?" I continued.

"Let me ask my dad." I heard Maddy shout through the phone, "Dad! Can I go to JP's house after school on Friday?"

"Yes, as long as you finish that science project by tomorrow," Mr. Rosenfeld responded.

"I'm already done, Dad." Maddy always finished her projects weeks in advance.

"Yep, J.P., I can come. What's this all about though? You never sound this amped, unless it's something really important."

"It involves Sylvester Sullivan, but I need to wait to tell you the rest."

"Okay. I guess I can wait. I'm curious though."

"You will know soon. See ya Friday."

"See ya!" Maddy hung up. Next call—Izzy.

"Hello?" Izzy picked up the phone on the first ring. That's because Izzy was ALWAYS on the phone, either texting or talking to someone. "Hey, Izzy!"

"Hi, chica! What's up?"

"Sofie and I have something really important to talk to you about. Can you come over on Friday right after school?"

"Let me check my schedule. Well, I have a meeting with the President of the United States at 4:30, but I guess I can cancel." Izzy loved to joke. It was very rare that you could catch her being serious about anything. Despite how much of a jokester she was, she was brilliant. Whenever Izzy had a task before her, she completed it with perfection.

"Thanks, Izzy."

"Alrighty! Catcha later!" She hung up quickly.

I turned around to Sofie. It was almost 4:30, and Sofie was getting ready to leave.

"Okay, JP. I think we're all set." Sofie seemed relieved that Izzy and Maddy were joining our team.

"I know we are. Sofie, we're going to change the world."

Sofie nodded in agreement, and we adjourned our meeting.

CHAPTER FIVE

It felt like a whole year passed before Friday came. I asked my grandmother to make extra baked goodies for our Friday meeting. In preparation for our meeting, my grandmother spent all week baking. By Friday, the kitchen was filled with pies, chocolate cakes, and chocolate chip cookies. After trying his best to stay away from them for two days, my grandfather finally gave in and snuck into the chocolate chip cookies on Thursday evening. Granny caught him, and gave him a scowl. "No more for you, sir! Those are for J.P. and my gals." Granny called Sofie, Izzy, and Maddy, her "gals."

Izzy was the first to arrive at my house on Friday afternoon. "Izzy!" I shouted as I opened the door. I was always surprised to see the latest ensemble that Izzy would be wearing. Izzy never wore the same outfit twice. To her, the worst thing that anyone could do was be remembered for wearing the same outfit more than once. What's more, she wore clothes that no one else wore because no one could find Izzy's clothes in regular stores. Izzy ordered all of her clothes from foreign countries, or made them herself.

Today, Izzy was wearing her jet-black hair in a bun that sat on top of her head, square in the center. She had recently dyed her bangs in streaks of red, yellow, blue, orange, and green, adding to her already unique style. Her white ruffled blouse looked as though she had borrowed it from the queen of the United Kingdom, but I had no idea where she had found her very exotic jeans. Her neon yellow jeans and matching tennis shoes were so bright that they almost required sunglasses to look at them.

"Is that my Isabelle?" I heard Granny ask from the kitchen. "Come in, honey. I made your favorite cookies."

"Izzy, it's because of you that Granny didn't let me get to these cookies. I'd be mad if she was saving these cookies for anyone but you." I heard Granddaddy come downstairs to the kitchen.

"Hey, Granny and Granddaddy! I've been waiting for these cookies all day!" Izzy loved my grandparents. She didn't know her biological parents or grandparents, because as a baby, Izzy had been adopted by her two dads. Her dads' parents died before she was born, so she never had the chance to meet them. Izzy was from a very poor town in South Korea. Her dads went to South Korea and brought her to the United States as soon as she was born.

Like Sofie, I met Izzy in the KLA law program when I was five years old. When I first met Izzy, she was doodling in her drawing pad. Izzy was the most talented artist that I knew. It always surprised me that she was a lawyer, because her first love was art. Maybe that's why she didn't get the best grades in law school. In our law program, Izzy was more interested in sketching out her next sculpture than she was studying the Constitution. Surprisingly, Izzy won the award for the best student investigator. Izzy could find out information on almost anything, and that's why I needed her on my team. If there were something about Sly that we didn't know, Izzy would find it.

As Izzy was busy chatting with my grandparents, I heard Maddy walk up to the door. "Maddy's here!" I shouted.

Maddy had been to my house a thousand times, but she always looked super confused when she was looking for my door. I could understand her confusion, because my neighborhood consisted of blocks of brick row homes that all looked identical. Maddy, however, didn't *only* seem confused finding my house. Every time I saw Maddy, she was frazzled about something.

Today, Maddy's red spiral curls were sprawled all over her head. Her large black-framed glasses were falling off, and her half-opened book bag was leaking loose sheets of paper. The gusty wind didn't help Maddy's composure. I decided to go outside and offer my friend some help getting to my house.

"Madeline Rosenfeld! You look like you need some help."

"Thanks, J.P.," Maddy responded, sounding defeated. "Let's get into your house. I'm freeeeeezing. It's 37 degrees right now, and the wind chill is 29 degrees. The rate of the wind speed will be increasing at a velocity of 10 miles per hour this afternoon."

Maddy was a math and science genius. She was another friend who I never would have expected to become a lawyer. Yet, Maddy loved using numbers to help her make legal arguments. Because of her gift with numbers, she was a great lawyer.

When I met Maddy, I noticed her in the corner of the cafeteria, sitting at lunch by herself. She was facing the cafeteria wall, and her bright red hair blended in with the red cafeteria mural. On the table in front of her sat a small notebook, a ruler, and two pencils. Maddy's head was bent towards her notebook, and her eyes were squinted, as if she were trying to focus her vision on something. I approached Maddy to ask her if she wanted to sit with Sofie, Izzy, and me. Izzy, Sofie, and I had been eating lunch together every day since our first day of law school.

"Sofie and Izzy, there's a girl from the law school sitting by herself. Let's go ask her if she wants to sit with us." I suggested. Sofie and Izzy followed me over to Maddy.

"Hi, I'm Juris, but people call me J.P. These are my two best friends, Sofie and Izzy. We were just wondering if you would like to sit with us." Maddy was still squinting off into space. I noticed that she was not eating lunch. She was drawing some complicated figure surrounded by numbers and strange lines.

Maddy finally looked up at me. "Nice to make your acquaintance, J.P. I'm working on my newest patent, but it would give me great pleasure to sit with you and your friends." I later learned that a "patent" was something that inventors got in order to protect their ideas from being stolen. Having a patent made someone's idea a piece of property, called intellectual property. Maddy was a patent genius—the master of intellectual property law.

Maddy stood up and walked to our table. When she stood up, she towered over Sofie, Izzy, and me. Her curly red hair gave her an extra inch of height on her already tall and slender frame. Maddy's face was sprinkled with freckles. We walked to our lunch table that day, and ever since, we have all been best friends.

Inside of my house, Granny was chatting with my friends about how she had gone apple picking last week and had used her apples to make her delicious treats. My friends listened closely as they sipped Granny's homemade apple cider. She had just taken an apple pie out of the oven, and the aroma of fresh apples and cinnamon hit Maddy and me as I opened the door to my house.

"Is that my Madeline?" I heard my grandmother shout from the kitchen.

"It is I, madam." Madeline responded. Granny came out of the kitchen with a piece of pie, so hot that you could see the steam rising from it. Granny knew all of my friends' favorite desserts, and apple pie was Maddy's.

"I made this just for you, honey." Granny welcomed Maddy, handing her a piece of warm pie.

"Okay, guys. We have to get this meeting started ASAP. We don't have time to waste." Sofie's parents had given her permission to be involved in this project, on the condition that she kept her grades up and always returned home by 5:00. Izzy and Maddy's parents had given them a 5:30 curfew, which didn't give us too much time to discuss my plan.

I led my friends to the basement, where Granddaddy had arranged four chairs around a small dark brown table. Granddaddy was building a more elegant table for me, but it would take at least another week for him to finish. When everyone was seated, I pulled out my notebook, which had all of the notes that I had been taking for the last week. I walked towards my chalkboard posted on the wall and pulled out a piece of chalk from my pocket.

"Friends, we are here today because we have two goals—one, to make sure that Sylvester does not get elected and two, getting kids the right to vote. Kids seven to seventeen years old that is." My friends looked up at me, listening attentively.

"Right to vote?" Izzy asked in disbelief.

"Yes, the right to vote," I repeated.

Sofie explained to Izzy and Maddy that Sylvester was horrible for children, and that the only way that his opponent, Marty Goodlittle, would win the election was if kids got the right to vote. Izzy and Maddy were obviously excited about the idea.

"How are we going to do this?" Maddy asked.

"Maddy, I need you to work out the numbers. How many kids do we need to vote for Goodlittle so that Sylvester does not get elected?"

Maddy rapidly punched some numbers into the calculator that seemed to be always glued to her hand. "Based on my calculations, we will need 7,052 votes from kids who are 8 to 17 to win this election for Marty Goodlittle."

"Thanks, Maddy."

"But *how* are we going to do this, J.P.?" asked Izzy. She wanted more details on exactly how we planned to get kids the right to vote. Izzy was a master investigator. I knew that when she asked that question, she had already brainstormed fifty questions that she planned on investigating. Her notepad with red and purple writing scribbled all over it confirmed this. Izzy's wheels were turning.

"We are going to have to use all of our knowledge, skills, and talents to make this happen. This is not going to be easy. We will face a number of challenges. Many people will tell us no. They will tell us that the law is that you have to be eighteen years old to vote. They will tell us that we are too young to change the law. They will tell us that kids should not have the right to vote. Many kids and their parents will not support this. But we *cannot* give up. We *cannot* listen to the people that don't believe in us. As long as we believe in ourselves, nothing else matters." My speech got slower, and my friends knew that when I began speaking slowly, I was serious.

Sofie interjected, "Ladies, we have to change the law, and we all know how hard that can be. It took several groups of Americans hundreds of years to get the right to vote. What we have to do is think creatively. We must convince people that this is important, and explain why it is illegal if kids don't have the right to vote."

"Of course we should have the right to vote. It's unconstitutional otherwise. I mean, equal protection means that everyone is equal under the law. We learned that in our constitutional law class," Maddy offered.

"Let's get down to business. We need a plan, and we need to make this plan work— quick, fast, and in a hurry." My voice was speeding up. I wrote the words "TO DO" on my chalkboard.

"Sofie, you are the best legal researcher out of all of us. You got an A+ in our legal research class during law school. You are going to be in charge of researching every legal argument for why kids should have the right to vote. Is that okay with you?"

"Yep!" Sofie responded proudly. Sofie knew that her greatest strength was legal research. I wrote "SOFIE LEGAL RESEARCH" in big, bold letters on my chalkboard.

"Onto you, Izzy. You know that you can investigate absolutely anything. We need to know everything about Sly, and I mean *everything*."

"You got it." Izzy asserted confidently. She stood up from her chair, walked over to me, and reached for my chalk. She wrote the words "IZZY—INVESTIGATE EVERYTHING~~~~ ☺ ☺." Izzy had to individualize everything with hearts and smiley faces. Izzy smiled with her head held high in the air as she walked back to the table.

"Okay. Last, but not least, our numbers whiz—
Maddy. Maddy, we need you to keep an eye on the numbers. We need to know who supports us,

how close we are to getting the support of people from this community to help us change the law. Any numbers that we need to know about, we need you to give them to us. Got it?"

"Got it!" I could see Maddy intensely squinting through her glasses. She was already thinking of her first major calculation. "What about you, J.P.? What's your role in all of this?"

"I've thought long and hard about all of this. First of all, even though we all have our individual tasks, we are a team. We will all help each other in any way that we can." Everyone nodded in agreement. "You all know that I love public speaking."

"Of course we know that," Sofie echoed. "You *are* the three time reigning champion of the KLA debate team."

"Well," I continued, "eventually, we will have to argue why kids should have the right to vote in front of a judge. I would like to be the one who makes the final argument, if that is okay with you guys."

"Fine with me."

"Of course!"

"No problem, J.P."

I had the support of my friends. "Thanks so much, guys! This means a lot to me. I'd also like to ask you one more thing." I looked at the clock on the table. We only had five more minutes before we had to wrap up the meeting. "If we are going to do this, I would like us to be a law firm. That means that nothing that any of us does is less important than what another person does. We all have an equal say in what goes on here." I could see everyone's eyes lighting up. When we were in law school, we all wanted to start our own law firm. I guess no one ever guessed that we would start it at eleven years old.

"J.P., this is a great idea. I think that the law firm should be named after you. What about the J.P. Firm?" Sofie asked.

"Hmmm… I think that it should be called J.P. & Associates." Maddy suggested.

"Ohhh… I love that name. It has a lot of spice!" Izzy remarked with a squeal.

"Okay, J.P. & Associates it is," I confirmed with a sense of pride that I had not felt since I graduated from law school. "Thanks so much, team. Let's get rollin'. I think that J.P. & Associates should meet every Friday after school here in the basement. How does that sound?"

"I will check with my parents, but I think that time works for me," Sofie responded.

"Same here," Izzy said.

"That should work, except in a couple months, it's my brother's bar mitzvah. My family and I will be pretty busy until then, but I will try my best to do all that I can to help," Maddy explained.

"Okay—let's plan for next Friday at 4:00." I wrote, "NEXT MEETING-FRIDAY 4:00 PM," on the chalkboard. "I will send everyone a reminder by email. Oh—and I guess I will see you at school." Everyone laughed.

My friends packed up their belongings, and I walked them to the door. Sofie's driver was waiting outside to take her home; Maddy and Izzy were walking to the metro station. I waved goodbye to everyone as they left, standing in my doorway as proud as a peacock.

I turned around to see Granddaddy sitting in his favorite chair, watching the evening news.

"How'd ya' meeting go, my little law-ya'?" My grandfather was from a small town called Kosciusko, Mississippi and had a deep southern accent.

"We started a law firm, Granddaddy! J.P & Associates! We are going to take Sly Sullivan down and get kids the right to vote."

"J.P & Associates. Well, ain't that something?" Granddaddy smiled in amusement. "You're doing a great thing, Juris. You know, you are a lucky gal. You have received a good education, and that means more than anything in the world. When I was ya' age, I wasn't allowed to go to the schools that you now attend because of the color of my skin. It was a different time back then, but it's because of law-ya's—brave law-ya's like yourself—that people of all colors and backgrounds can have a fair chance to get an education and do anything that they want to do in life. You and ya' friends can change the world, all because of a little thing called knowledge."

I loved hearing my grandfather's stories about when he was a child. They painted pictures of an unfamiliar world, where the opportunities that I have today were non-existent.

"You know, Juris. Your mother would be so proud of ya'." I turned the volume on the television down. My grandparents rarely talked about my mother. She died a few weeks after I was born, and I did not remember anything about her. My aunts and uncles told me that, after she died, everyone in my family was so sad that my grandparents took most of her

pictures down and placed all of her belongings
in boxes in our attic. I was always afraid to ask
about my mother because I did not want to upset
my grandparents. Every time someone spoke
about my mother, I drank each of their words in
as if they provided water for an insatiable thirst.

"Ya' mother wanted to be a law-ya', but
when she got married, she decided to devote her
time to working and preparing to be a motha'."

Granddaddy's words made me wonder about
who my mother was. Was I like her? Did I look
like her? Did I talk like her? Would she be
proud of me? Did she like being a mom?

"She always wanted to go to law school.
That's all she talked about, law school this and
law school that. She went to college in a little
town called Charlottesville, down in Virginia.
As soon as she finished college, she wanted to
go to law school in Charlottesville, but she
decided to work at a law firm to get experience
before applying to law school. Before having
you, she worked at the law firm of Baker and
Phelps, and boy, did she love it. She would
come home each day and tell us about all of the
interesting people that she would see in court,
and how she could not wait until she was a real
law-ya'."

I tried to picture the excitement that my mother must have felt by working in a law firm. Did she feel as excited as I felt by having my own firm?

"Every night, she would stay up until the wee hours of the morning to do research on her cases for the next day at work. She never seemed to get tired of it," Granddaddy continued.

My mom reminded me a lot of myself. I could stay up all night researching a case that I was passionate about.

"Each morning, she would dress up in her black suit, and on the way out of the door, she would grab her pink leather briefcase, which had the research that she had done the night before."

My grandfather explained that he and my grandmother searched the whole city for a pink briefcase because pink was my mother's favorite color. I smiled brightly because pink was also my favorite color.

"We couldn't really afford it, but your grandmother and I bought your mother that briefcase with the last dime of our paychecks right before she started that law firm job. We wanted your mother to feel like she was the best employee in the law firm. She never went anywhere without her briefcase," Granddaddy recalled.

"Why not?" I asked curiously.

"She always told me and your grandmother that the briefcase made her feel like a real law-ya', and that made us so happy." Granddaddy's face showed his sadness as he recounted fond memories of my mother. "Juris, hold on one second."

I sat quietly in the living room, reflecting on what Granddaddy had told me about my mother. I would give anything that I had in the world to be in my mother's presence for just ten minutes.

"Juris, I'd like you to have somethin'." Granddaddy was standing in the archway of the living room holding a pink leather briefcase. On a small, square silver tag hanging from the handle of the briefcase, the words "J. P. Prudence" were engraved. JoAnn Parnell Prudence. Sometimes, I could overhear my grandparents talking about "Ann" when they thought that I was asleep. I wondered who "Ann" was for many years, and one day, I finally gathered the courage to ask my grandmother who "Ann" was. She told me that "Ann" was my mother.

"Ann would have liked you to have this. You are the law-ya' that she always wanted to be."

Granddaddy carefully handed me the briefcase, holding it as delicately as someone would hold a newborn baby.

"Granddaddy. I can't take this." I was overwhelmed with emotion.

"Your grandmother and I have been waitin' to give this to you, Juris. We think that now is the time."

I reached for the briefcase and placed it on my shoulder carefully. Carrying my mother's most prized possession made me feel closer to her. Graduating from law school did not make me feel like a real lawyer. Even having my new law firm did not make me feel like a real lawyer. But, something about this briefcase made me believe that I was actually a lawyer who could change the law. I guess I was like my mother in more ways than I knew.

CHAPTER SIX

J.P. & Associates wasted no time beginning our mission to get kids the right to vote. The election was approaching, and we had a bunch of work to do. My best friends and I didn't have any classes together, so it was difficult to talk to each other during the school day. On Thursdays, we had lunch together, but today was Tuesday, and there was a ton to be done before our next meeting this Friday.

Between classes, I ran into Izzy. "J.P., are you still able to do that thing we talked about yesterday?" Izzy had told me and the rest of J.P. & Associates that we had to keep our investigation of Sly completely confidential until we completed the investigation. Izzy would only refer to the investigation as the "thing."

"Yes. My debate team practice is over at four today. Can we go after that?"

"That's cool. This place closes at 5:00, so we will have to hurry." Izzy would not use Sly's name in conversation. She had already begun her research about Sly, and I could see by the intense look in her eyes that she had a very clear purpose for whatever we were about to do this afternoon.

"Are you sure you can't tell me where we're going today?"

"Nope. Just trust me." Izzy knew that, out of everyone in our law firm, I was the person most likely to go along with her zany ideas. Izzy threw me a shopping bag. "Put this on immediately after your debate practice."

I looked inside the bag and discovered a janitor's uniform. "Um... Izzy, what is this?" I could not hide the apprehension in my voice.

"J.P., you have to trust me. It's something I made last night. Just put it on. I gotta get to my literature class, but I'll see ya' this afternoon. Meet me at my locker at 4:00 sharp!"

With that, Izzy turned around and darted down the hall. Before I could say "okay," all I could see was her midnight black ponytail and hot pink hair tie vanishing down the hallway.

****

The day moved quickly. Before I knew it, debate practice was over, and it was time for me to meet Izzy. Running into the bathroom, I rushed to change into my janitor's uniform.

During our law school days, I would often catch Izzy drawing elaborate outfits in her notebook. As we became closer friends, she told me that she had a secret hobby of sewing the outfits that she sketched. Her dads wanted her to focus on law school, so she would get in trouble whenever they caught her sewing instead of doing her homework. Izzy had a closet full of outfits that had come right out of her sketchpad. The unique designs on the janitor's uniform allowed me to make no mistake that this was a uniform that Izzy had drawn and sewn.

Following Izzy's instructions, I met her at her locker at four, fully dressed in my uniform.

"You look great, J.P, or should I say, 'Sue'?" Izzy joked. Izzy and I were matching in our khaki brown pants, and identical khaki brown shirts, with our sewn name badges. Between her art classes and her school obligations, I had no idea how Izzy had managed to find time to create a baseball cap that complemented our uniforms. Today, I was "Sue," and apparently, Izzy was "Kathy."

"Okay, Izzy. What the heck are we doing?"

"Let's walk and talk, Sue." Izzy rapidly walked out of the school building in the direction of the metro, and I quickly followed her. In almost a whisper, she explained our plan. "We need to get a glimpse into the subject's life. We need to go onto his territory. That's the only way we will know who he really is."

"What do you mean? Who is 'the subject,' Iz?" I asked in confusion.

"Sly is 'the subject.' We're going to his office, J.P. And, by the way, my name is Kathy." Izzy whispered to me, not wanting to say Sly's name out loud.

"Oh man...."

"Don't worry. We'll be fine. I have been scoping out the subject's office for the past few days. Each afternoon, at 4:30, he comes outside of the office building to dump his own trash into the public dumpsters. His trash is always in a bright red bag."

I nodded, hanging on to Izzy's every word.

"The garbage disposal truck comes to empty the trash bins at exactly 4:45 every afternoon. When the garbage truck driver comes to empty the trash bin this afternoon, we will ask the driver if we can have the trash in the red bag. Hopefully, he will say yes. If he says no, we are out of luck, my dear Sue."

"All of the janitors wear the uniforms that we have on. They leave the office around 4:30 and many of them hang out in the back of the building, where we will be waiting for the subject to dump his trash. We will fit right in, other than the fact that we will be a little shorter than everyone else, but hey, who cares, right?"

"Right…." I responded hesitantly. I was terrified that we would be discovered.

"Just keep your baseball cap on. If anyone sees our faces, they will know that we do not belong around the office. In that case, we might be in some hot water, my friend. This is a very dangerous task. We don't want the subject to know that we're on to him. "

"Once we get to the building, we can't talk to each other. We need to split up. Here's a map of the building. I've circled the area that you need to watch. I've got the other area. We need to stay outside of the building and watch for the subject. He doesn't always dump his trash in the same dumpster."

"What does the star mean here?" I asked, pointing to the map.

"That's the dumpster where the subject dumped his trash yesterday," Izzy replied. "You will be casing out that dumpster."

"Me?"

"Yes, you, Sue." Izzy sarcastically replied. Izzy handed me a box full of trash bags.

"What do I do with these?"

"Sue, you are a janitor. You pick up trash."

"Oh, yea." I felt silly for already forgetting my role.

"Keep your eyes and ears open. Listen for statements about the subject that we can use against him. We are looking for evidence. Understand?"

"Got it," I replied. As we stepped onto the metro train, butterflies were going crazy in my stomach, but I knew that I couldn't back out, especially because this was my idea.

"Oh, I almost forgot to tell you the most important thing. These aren't regular uniforms." Izzy mischievously chuckled as she uttered the words. Izzy then took off her baseball cap. "I went to the spy store the other day and picked up a few things."

"You went to the what?" I asked in shock. Izzy always went the extra mile when she was assigned with a task, and I shouldn't have put this past her.

"On the top of our caps, there's a secret camera. It will record everything we see." Izzy pointed to a brown plastic circle, the size of a dime, which was located on the brim of the baseball cap I was wearing. I didn't notice it until Izzy pointed it out. "One more thing—there's a camera inside of your sunglasses. If you need to take a picture of anything, just press on the right side of the sunglasses. Okay?"

I nodded, feeling a bit overwhelmed by the thought of all that we had to accomplish this afternoon. During our train ride, I was quiet as I watched Izzy dance wildly to the sounds coming through her headphones. Izzy always acted as though she did not have a care in the world. On the other hand, I sat in my seat, frantic about how we were going to carry out this plan to get vital information about Sly. I knew I had to trust Izzy though. After all, I had put her in charge of investigations because I knew that she was the best person for the job.

"Metro Center!" The conductor of the train exclaimed. We had reached our stop. It was game time.

"Sue, let's go." Izzy was in character.

"Okay, Kathy. I'm ready," I replied confidently.

There was no turning back now. As planned, we approached the city hall building and each went to our separate locations outside of the building.

A swarm of people came in and out of the building, discussing the upcoming election.

"Did you throw away those documents as we discussed?!" a gray-haired man yelled to a man walking beside him.

"I wasn't able to do it today." The man seemed terrified.

"Do it now! Now, I said!" the gray-haired man shouted rudely.

I noticed that the gray-haired man had a name tag that read, "Gary Sullivan, Chief of Staff." This morning, I read in the newspaper that Gary Sullivan was Sylvester Sullivan's son. Supposedly, he had dropped out of college, and his dad had hired him to manage his first mayoral campaign. The newspaper report said that he had a long criminal record, but it did not say what he had done to get in trouble.

Gary continued yelling at the man outside of the city hall building as he walked towards the dumpster where I was hiding. I checked my baseball cap to make sure that my video camera was recording all that I was seeing.

As Gary was heading back inside of the city hall building, he stopped at the entrance of building to make a call on his cell phone. "Hi 'C' this is Gary. Did you handle that thing that we talked about yesterday?" Gary asked covertly. I wondered who "C" was and what this "thing" was. Whatever Gary was discussing, it was something he wanted to keep a secret.

As I daydreamed about all of the useful information I was capturing, my thoughts were suddenly interrupted.

"Sue!" Gary shouted.

I was crouched over in a corner beside the dumpster recording Gary's conversation when I heard my code-name. I couldn't believe that he could see my name-tag from where he was standing. I guess I wasn't standing as far away from Gary as I thought I was.

"I'm not S—" I almost forgot my new identity, but I rapidly got back into my character.

"Hi," I replied, mortified that my true identity had been discovered.

"Sue, yesterday, my trash was not emptied! You need to make sure that each trashcan in that building is empty every day. I can't have food rotting in my office and smelling like a pigsty the next day. We have real business taking place around here."

"I'm sorry, sir." I kept my head bent down as I answered.

"You're sorry? Is that all you can say?"

"It won't happen again." I hoped that this response was enough to get me off the hook so that I could get away from him as fast as possible.

"Are you new? I've never seen you here before? And what are you, like ten years old? I really don't understand where they find you people. Goodness, we gotta do something about this. How many times have I told them that we need new cleaning people in this office?" I sat quietly and let Gary rant, hoping that he would get tired of hearing himself talk and let me leave. "Just get outta here."

Happily, I obeyed his wishes. I practically sprinted to the other side of the building, in hopes of finding Izzy to tell her about my encounter with Gary. In the midst of running to meet Izzy, I looked down at my watch and noticed that it was 4:45, and I still had not seen Sly dump his trash. My heart was racing out of panic.

Just when I thought my heartbeat had slowed down, it sped back up. I was so focused on finding Izzy that I almost ran into a man holding a bright red bag. I stopped dead in my tracks as I realized that the man was wearing a nametag that read, "SYLVESTER SULLIVAN, MAYOR." Seeing his name sent chills down my spine. Sylvester Sullivan was anxiously looking around the building, as if he were waiting for someone. glaring at me through his square, narrow reading glasses.

"May I help you, kid?!" Sylvester shouted when he noticed me looking up at him.

"Just picking up the trash." I truthfully admitted, with my voice quivering.

Sylvester kept staring, as if he was waiting for me to say more.

I could tell that Sylvester was suspicious of me lurking around the office building. As I started picking up trash from off the ground, I could feel his eyes glued to me. My hands were shaking as I reached for his an aluminum can on the ground. The shaking got so bad that I couldn't grip the sides of the can.

"Kid, you don't know how to pick up trash? Isn't that your job?" Sylvester noticed my nervousness, and I hoped with all of my heart that my true identity would not be discovered.

"Sorry," I replied, keeping my head down so that Sylvester could not see my face.

"You don't look like you're old enough to be a sanitation worker."

I did not respond.

"I don't believe that kids can do anything that is going to help the world, including picking up trash. That's what we have adults for." Sylvester spoke right into the video recorder on my baseball cap. Despite how scared I was, I knew that I was capturing some great footage that would help the law firm's campaign to get kids the right to vote.

"I mean really, how old are you? You can't be more than twelve years old. You must be in some kind of special program that lets you work here, because you couldn't work at this office being your age unless you have special permission. I'm going to make sure that this program is stopped. It's clearly not working. You can't even pick up trash properly. Stupid kids. You make my life so difficult," Sly continued on his tirade.

"Anything else you want to say, Sly?" I realized that I was getting mad, but I needed to rein myself in. It was very important that I stay in character.

"Did you call me, Sly? My name is Mayor Sullivan to you, kiddo. Get out of here, and don't you ever come back."

Luckily, this was my last day on janitor duty. Still feeling Sly's eyes staring me down, I ran to the side of the building and peeked around the corner in order to watch to see where Sly threw away his red trash bag.

After I saw Sly toss his red bag into the dumpster and return to the city hall building, I ran to the dumpster to wait for the garbage truck driver. It seemed like it took a decade for the truck driver to arrive, but when he finally did, I immediately pleaded, "Can I please have the trash that is in the red garbage bag?!"

"Pardon me, young lady?" The driver was understandably confused.

"I really need that red trash bag, sir." I stated desperately.

"Okay. If you say so. Enjoy." The driver handed me the bag nonchalantly.

"Thank you so much, sir!" I said graciously.

The time was now 5:00, and it was time for me to meet Izzy. I was excited about the statements that Sly had made on my video, and I couldn't wait to share them with Izzy.

****

Sofie had returned from her student council meeting early and, unlike most days, she did not have any homework that day, probably because Sofie liked to do most of her homework days in advance. Sofie's parents would not arrive at home from their doctors' rounds at the hospital until late that night. It was the perfect time for Sofie to start her legal research.

"Would you like some hot tea, my dear Sofia?" Maria asked gently. Maria had lived with Sofie's family since Sofie was a baby, and she helped take care of Sofie and her brother. Each day, while Sofie was studying, she would bring Sofie a warm drink.

"Sure," Sofie happily replied. Maria knew how much Sofie missed her parents on the days they were working late. Sofie's parents worked late at least four nights a week. Maria tried her best to take Sofie's mind off of her parents being gone, but she knew how much Sofie disliked them being gone several nights in a row.

Today, however, Sofie's mind was focused on researching the vote, which took her mind off of her parents working. Grabbing her laptop, Sofie began her research. She typed "Fourteenth Amendment," "Fifteenth Amendment," and "Vote" into the search engine. Sofie smiled brightly when the she saw the first two results from her search—*Guinn v. United States* and *Lane v. Wilson.* She remembered studying these cases in law school, and she knew that these cases would be extremely important in helping kids get the right to vote.

A number of other legal cases popped up as Sofie continued her research, and she knew that it would be a long night reading those cases and taking notes about them for our next meeting. Looking at the names of those cases reminded Sofie of when she learned about women's right to vote during law school. When Sofie first learned that, at one time, women could go to jail for trying to vote, she was shocked. One woman, Susan B. Anthony, had actually tried to vote with her three sisters and other women, but police arrested them and took them to jail before they could cast their votes. *How could adult women not be able to vote?* Sofie thought.

Sofie continued researching cases until she finally looked up from her computer, and the clock read 11:00 p.m. She had been immersed in research for hours, and it was past her bedtime. Before Sofie went to bed, she wanted to tell her parents about the interesting cases that she'd found. Sofie's parents usually arrived home by 9:30 on the nights that they worked late at the hospital. Noticing that her parents had not arrived home yet, Sofie ran into Maria's room to ask where her parents were. Maria was busy putting away Sofie's brother's laundry.

"Maria?" Sofie asked softly.

"Sí, mi amor," Maria responded. Maria knew that Sofie would be asking where her parents were, as this was what Sofie did every time her parents were late getting home.

"Donde están mama y papa?" Sofie asked.

Maria responded that Sofie's mom and dad had called earlier to inform Maria that they would be working until midnight at the hospital and that they would be home before Sofie went to school the next morning.

"Oh. Okay," Sofie replied, disappointed. Sofie understood that her parents were saving lives, but she couldn't help but feel upset when they weren't around. She longed to share the events of her day with them. Often, Sofie felt like my grandmother and Maria knew her better than her own parents. Sofie called my house. She knew it was late, but she needed to talk to someone.

Granny answered the phone.

"Hi, Granny!" Sofie exclaimed, so excited that Granny answered.

"Hi, honey. What are you doing up so late? I know your parents do not let you stay up past ten o'clock."

"They're not here," Sofie sadly responded.

"Well, I'm sure they will be home soon," Granny cheerfully replied.

"I guess so...." Sofie obviously did not believe that her parents would be back anytime soon.

"How was your day, honey?" Granny knew that Sofie loved talking about what was going on in her classes and student council.

Sofie's voice immediately perked up. "Student Council is planning a fundraiser, and if we raise $500, the principal will sit on a chair and let us throw a pie in his face."

"Oh my, honey. That sounds very exciting. Good luck!"

"Thanks, Granny. Can I please talk to J.P. for a few minutes? I promise I won't be long."

"All right. I'll give y'all five minutes. J.P., telephone! It's Sofia."

I ran downstairs to pick up the phone. "Hey, Sofie!"

"Hi, J.P., I found some great cases for us!" I could hear the excitement in Sofie's voice.

"Awesome! Can you bring the team copies for our meeting on Friday?"

"No problem!"

"Well, it looks like we have a lot to discuss on Friday. Izzy and I have to share what we discovered today. I think we've got some good stuff too."

"Perfect. Well, can't wait to hear all about it on Friday," Sofie responded happily.

"Sounds good. Talk to you tomorrow."

We had accomplished a lot in one day—we'd gathered evidence and found great cases. More importantly, we had made the first major moves towards ending Sly's reign in the city. I considered this day a success.

CHAPTER SEVEN

Our next Friday meeting approached faster than I expected. We had accomplished so much during the week—a scope out of Sly's office, a massive amount of legal research, and the formation of our firm. I couldn't wait for the girls to reconvene to share what we had done and to come up with our next steps.

The morning of our meeting, I asked Granny to whip up her specialties—chocolate chip cookies and sweet potato pie. Granny knew that she had special orders to keep Granddaddy away from the goodies.

That morning, I jumped on my bike, soaking in the crisp fall breeze. I snapped my bright pink helmet on and embraced the wind flowing through my hair as I coasted to school. On my journey, I took in the sights and sounds of the city, from the farmers' markets to the majestic site of the Washington Monument. As I rode my bike through the city, I wondered, *is it possible that my firm can really be the force that radically changes the rights for kids in this city?* The mere possibility exhilarated me. I contemplated the answer to that question, as my bike trekked through the city.

Before I knew it, I had arrived at the Kids Leaders Academy. I locked up my bike at the bike stand outside of KLA and headed into school. To my surprise, I was twenty minutes early that morning.

Instead of hanging out by my locker to wait to talk to Izzy, Maddy, and Sofie, I decided to go straight to class and check over my homework before turning it in. When I got to class, I noticed that I was the first student to arrive. *Here we go again,* I thought to myself. *Another awkward moment with Nitpick Nicholson.*

"Good morning, Miss Prudence. You're here mighty early."

"Yes, ma'm. Just wanted to check over my homework."

"Very good, Miss Prudence. I appreciate such diligence in a student."

The firm's efforts to get voting rights for kids had renewed my passion for learning about the history behind voting rights in America. Today, the students in my class were making a presentation on the most important developments in voting rights. I chose to discuss the Voting Rights Act of 1965. As I waited for class to start, I looked over my presentation notes.

Students gradually trickled into the class. The poster boards and diagrams that they had created for their presentations amazed me. Glancing around the room, I saw the names Sojourner Truth, Susan B. Anthony, Martin Luther King, Jr., and Fannie Lou Hamer. I had studied these people in law school, but it had been ages since I had learned about them. I was looking forward to hearing my classmates' presentations so that I could refresh my memory about these awesome historical figures.

The bell rung, and Ms. Nicholson immediately started class. "Good morning, class. All week, I've looked forward to the presentations that I know that you have been working on for the past several weeks. Do we have any volunteers to begin our presentations?" Ms. Nicholson scanned the room with her eyes. I kept my head down; I did not want to go first.

"Miss Prudence, let's hear from you."

"Gosh," I mumbled under my breath. I never liked going first. I gathered the poster board that

I had created, and handed out small diagrams to my classmates so that they could follow my presentation.

"Good morning, class. I will be presenting on the Voting Rights Act of 1965. President Lyndon B. Johnson passed the Voting Rights Act of 1965. This law was passed during the Civil Rights Movement. The Civil Rights Movement was a period in American history, in which African- Americans fought for their rights to equality." I paused to let the class absorb what I was saying. I'd been on the debate team at KLA since I was five years old, so I was used to speaking in front of large groups.

"One of the rights that African-Americans had to fight for was the right to vote. African-Americans who voted risked their lives. They were often beaten, arrested, and harassed when trying to cast their ballots. In 1965, President Johnson signed the Voting Rights Act that made it illegal to prohibit any group from exercising its right to vote.

Caleb Patterson raised his hand. "Yes, Caleb?" I said, acknowledging his question. "Why did President Johnson feel the need to pass a *law* to protect people's right to vote? Didn't the law already allow *everyone* to vote?"

"I'm glad you asked that question," I responded, turning to the diagram that I had made. "That brings me to my next point. During the Civil Rights Movement, many groups did not believe that African-Americans should have the right to vote. In order to stop them from voting, these groups would go to the polls where voting would occur and use violence to keep African-Americans from voting. Many African-Americans were killed or severely injured for trying to vote." With my pointer, I directed the class to a sign that read "March 7, 1965."

I continued speaking, "March 7, 1965 was a monumental moment leading up to the passage of the Voting Rights Act. On this day, a group of protestors who were marching in support of voting equality participated in a peaceful march on the Edmund Pettus Bridge in Selma, Alabama. As the marchers made their way across the bridge, they encountered a huge group of police officers that were carrying bats and tear gas. The marchers were brutally beaten by the police. The whole country saw images of the peaceful marchers who had been beaten for trying to get the right to vote.

"The same year as the march, the Voting Rights Act was signed by President Lyndon B. Johnson." On my diagram, I pointed to a picture of President Johnson. "The Voting Rights Act is one of the most significant civil rights laws because of the people that risked their lives to make sure that people have the rights that this law guarantees. If no one has any questions, that is the end of my presentation." I concluded.

"Very nicely done, Miss Prudence. Does anyone have any further questions for Miss Prudence?" Ms. Nicholson asked the class. No one raised a hand.

"Well, I have one question, Miss Prudence," Ms. Nicholson stated.

I nodded, waiting for whatever question Ms. Nicholson was about to throw my way.

"What role does the Voting Rights Act play in today's society?" Ms. Nicholson lowered her head and looked at me over her narrow glasses.

I paused, reflecting on my answer before I responded. "The Voting Rights Act is important in today's society because there are still many groups of people that are not allowed to vote. Kids, for example. Voting is a fundamental right in this country. Everyone should have an equal right to vote, regardless of his or her age, color, class, or background. The Voting Rights Act reminds us of this right."

"Kids, any further questions? Very informative, Miss Prudence. Thank you." Ms. Nicholson rarely gave compliments, so I gladly accepted her compliment and quickly gathered my presentation materials.

The class clapped, and I sat down, relieved that I had finished my presentation. As my classmates presented, I tried my best to listen intently, but I kept drifting off. I wanted 4:00 to get there as soon as humanly possible. I needed to find out what the firm had accomplished this week. After all, the election was right around the corner.

We had time for five presentations. At the end of the fifth presentation, the bell rung, and it was time for lunch. Today was a special day at KLA. This was the first day that we were allowed to leave the KLA campus for lunch. Last year, Sofie introduced an initiative in student council that would give KLA students the chance to eat lunch away from the KLA campus every Thursday. The KLA principal was hesitant to go along with this idea, but Sofie convinced our principal that eating lunch away from school would make students happier, and happier students have more energy to study and make good grades.

I met Maddy, Sofie, and Izzy at my locker. The previous day we had decided to go our favorite restaurant near the school, the Good Times Deli. The afternoon was just as beautiful as the morning had been. The bright sun and the crisp breeze made the autumn air perfect. Deep brown, green, red, yellow, and orange hews from the fallen leaves surrounded Georgetown where our school was located and reminded us that summer was gone, and autumn had arrived.

We walked a short two blocks to the deli, chatting about our classes earlier that day. "Can you believe that Ms. Humphries had lipstick on her teeth during the entire class?" Izzy gossiped as we walked down the street.

"Stop gossiping, Izzy. Ms. Humphries is my favorite teacher." Sofie responded.

Maddy and I quietly giggled.

We approached the deli, anxious to order, as we were all starving. The deli had great sandwiches, salads, and fruit smoothies. They also had tables outside, facing the Potomac River. We loved sitting outside by the water, and today was the perfect day for it. "This is the best lunch time ever. Way to go, Sofie!"

"Yea, Sofie!" Maddy and Izzy echoed.

We all gave Sofie a high five to congratulate her on the successful lunchtime initiative. As we all chatted about how excited we were to be able to eat something other than KLA cafeteria food, we stepped up to the deli counter. I ordered my usual tuna fish sandwich and vanilla milkshake, my favorite items off of the deli menu. Izzy ordered a salad off of the vegetarian menu, while Maddy and Sofie ordered chicken salad sandwiches and berry smoothies.

"J.P. and Izzy, I can't wait to hear what you've found out about Sly," Maddy expressed.

I choked on my milkshake. "Maddy, we can't discuss him in public! We've got to keep this under wraps until we've got enough information about 'you know who'—information that would support our efforts to get us the right to vote. If 'you know who' finds out that we are attempting to change voting laws in favor of kids, he would doom us!"

"She's right, Maddy. He's dangerous. Very dangerous. I will tell you more when we meet tomorrow, but I've found out some things that make it very important that this project stays between us *and only us* until we know that we can win this fight. If we don't, we may be in danger," Izzy emphasized.

As Izzy talked, I could feel the tension mounting in the air. We had never considered the fact that what we were doing had the potential of putting us in danger. I was confident in our efforts, but I did not want to put my friends or myself in danger. Noticing the worry that was plastered on everyone's faces, I decided to change the subject. It wasn't worth wasting our few moments of freedom from campus on worrying about something over which we had no control.

"Maddy, did you get your dress for your brother's bar mitzvah?" I asked, attempting to clear the air.

"Yea, I don't like it though. My mom wants me and Ava to match. I told her that just because we're identical twins, it doesn't mean that we always have to wear matching clothing. It's not like we're four years old anymore."

Maddy's identical twin sister, Ava, was the polar opposite of Maddy. Their faces were the only things that they had in common. Ava wore makeup and straightened her curly red hair every day. She loved dressing in the latest designer clothing and wearing matching purses and jewelry. Maddy, on the other hand, couldn't care less about her hair or clothing, and she usually wore Ava's hand me downs. Maddy's parents often had to hound Ava about her academic performance, as Ava cared more about her appearance than her grades. Contrarily, Maddy's parents only hounded Maddy about coming out of her home science lab and going shopping more. Maddy despised being compared to her sister. Even more, she detested dressing like her sister.

"I just can't wait for the whole day to be over. I'm wearing the dress just to make my parents happy. Ava picked out the dress, as usual," Maddy complained.

"I'm sure you will look beautiful in it, Maddy," Sofie tried to assure her.

My attempt at lightening the mood wasn't going so well, so I tried again. "Guess what, guys, KLA Day is coming up soon! I can't wait!" KLA Day was the best day in the school year.

All semester, kids looked forward to this day. KLA Day was filled with games, prizes, and presentations about what students had accomplished during the semester. Teachers did not give any homework the night before KLA Day. The day was pure fun.

"OMG! KLA Day is going to be great! Student Council is planning a huge cookout. We're having a bake sale and giving all of the money that we raise to a homeless shelter in D.C. We haven't decided which one yet. Do you guys want to bake something to contribute to the sale?" Sofie perked up.

"Sure!"

"No prob!"

"Yep!"

We all agreed to contribute to the bake sale. "I'll ask Granny to make a couple of her famous pies. I know that they'll be a best-seller." Granny's baked goods were a hit at KLA. At least once a year, I brought some pies to share with my classmates at KLA. I would always run out of food within the first hour that I arrived at school. That's just how good Granny's food was.

"That would be great, J.P.!" Sofie exclaimed. "The class that raises the most money gets to throw a pie in Principal Marshall's face. We also just learned that the winning class gets to go on a trip to the White House!" The White House was Sofie's favorite place in Washington. She had never told anyone except for me, but she dreamed of being the President of the United States one day. She loved being a leader.

"I hope our class wins! I want to pie Mr. Marshall, and going to the White House will be a-ma-zing! Do you think we will get to see the President?" Izzy cheerfully asked.

"I sure do hope so," Sofie responded. "We have to win first."

"We will," I asserted with confidence. "With Granny's pies, we have this in the bag."

"Okay, ladies," Sofie glanced down at her watch. "We've got to hurry up and finish eating. We only had an hour for lunch, and we were closely approaching the hour mark. It was time for us to head back to campus. We quickly gobbled down our sandwiches, and got up to walk back to KLA. As Izzy, Sofie, and Maddy continued to discuss KLA Day, I was quiet, preoccupied with Izzy's comments about the danger that we may have put ourselves in by starting our crusade against Sly. Although it was Thursday, waiting until Friday would be torture; I was both curious and nervous to find out what further information Izzy had discovered about

Sly. More importantly, I wanted to know what danger we might be in.

CHAPTER EIGHT

Our Friday firm meeting had finally arrived. I spent all night last night thinking of what Izzy had possibly found that would make her think that we were in danger. Did Sly know what we were doing? How would he know? Had he noticed us the day that we were scoping out his office? All day, my heart was racing. After my final class, I sped towards my bike, popped on my helmet, and peddled home as fast as I could.

When I walked in, Granny's "hello honey" hit my ears at the same time that the smell of her sweet potato pie hit by nose. Granny now looked forward to our Friday meetings. She loved cooking, and our meetings gave her the chance to make all of her favorite treats.

"What time are the gals coming?" Granny asked as she walked out of the kitchen. Granny's apron was covered in flour. White puffs of flour covered her round, brown cheeks.

I could tell that she had been working hard preparing for our meeting.

"They'll be here at four, Granny."

"Oh my!" Granny looked panicked. "I got to hurry up then. I only have ten minutes! I was making y'all some strawberry lemonade, and I've got to go squeeze my lemons." Granny's fresh made strawberry lemonade was a real treat. Granny did not use any sugar in it but, somehow, it tasted perfectly sweet.

"Granny, I'm going to head downstairs to our office. Please just tell the girls to come down here when they get here."

"All right, honey."

I went downstairs to the basement, which Granddaddy had completely transformed into our firm office. He had built a long, round table with four chairs around it. On the door to the basement, Granddaddy had created a sign, engraved with the words, "Juris P. Prudence & Associates." Our chalkboard was affixed to the wall, and Granny had placed legal pad notebooks and pens at each place at the table. We were a real law firm, and I could not have been prouder.

As I was admiring our office, I heard Izzy shout downstairs, "What's up J to the P? Are you ready to rock and roll?"

"Hey, Iz! You have to tell me what danger you were referring to yesterday! I couldn't sleep all night! I've been thinking about it all day! Please, Izzy... Tell me!" I pleaded uncontrollably.

"Whoa." Izzy responded, unmoved. "J.P., get a hold of yourself, girlie. I have to wait until Sofie and Maddy get here before I say anything about our work. We are a firm. That means we work together. We are a team. Does that sound familiar? I believe it was you who said that just a little while ago." Izzy's sarcasm was one of her most charming and annoying traits.

"You're right. I just want to know what we're up against," I replied.

"I can't wait to taste some of Granny's pie." Izzy was also very good at ignoring people.

As Izzy hopped up the stairs to retrieve some of Granny's pie, Maddy and Sofie trickled in. "Are we late?" Sofie asked. "Traffic was terrible getting here. My driver took the quickest route that he knew." Sofie and Maddy had ridden over together from school because they both had after school meetings that day.

"Did you guys grab some lemonade and pie?" I asked.

"Don't worry, I'll bring it down." Granny could overhear me from upstairs.

"Thanks, Granny!" Sofie, Maddy, Izzy, and I responded in unison.

"Let's get started," I commanded. "A lot has happened since the last time that we all got together. Should we go around the table one by one and get updates from everyone?"

"Let's do it," Izzy responded. "You start, J.P."

"Okay, well, first off-Izzy and I completed a stake-out of Sly's office."

"You did what?!" Sofie interrupted.

"Umm … yea … we kinda disguised ourselves in janitors uniforms and scoped out Sly's office. When he threw his trash in the dumpster outside of his office building, we asked the dump truck driver if we could have it, and he said "yes." We needed something to prove that he shouldn't be reelected because he doesn't like kids," I continued.

"Oh my….." Sofie looked perplexed. Our stake out of Sly's office was obviously not something that she approved.

"So, what did you find?" Maddy chimed in.

"I'm getting to that…." I responded. "Sly was incredibly rude, to everyone—his staff, me— everyone." I repeated. "We were outside of his office building for less than a half hour, and it was clear that he is not someone to be crossed. I collected stuff out of the trash he discarded, but I didn't have time to go through it. I gave all of the trash that I collected to Izzy. Iz, take it from here."

"I must say that I admire anyone who picks up trash all day. That's the hardest job that I've ever had," Izzy started.

"I agree. That was hard work," I confirmed.

"Well, brace yourselves, guys. I carefully went though the evidence."

"You mean trash?" Maddy clarified.

"Not trash—evidence." Izzy reached into her backpack and pulled out four plastic locked sandwich bags. "Here's what I've found. Please don't take anything out of the baggies." Izzy passed the baggies around the table one by one.

"Exhibit A—Sly's telephone records. Please take note of line three—a call to Marvin Cromwell, an inmate at the Washington, D.C. jail. Sentenced for child kidnapping."

We all passed the first bag around in silence.

Izzy pulled the next plastic bag from her backpack. "Exhibit B—Sly's probation report."

"Probation?!" we shouted at the same time.

"Yes," Izzy explained. "In 1976, Sly was convicted of kidnapping a child and putting the child to work in his clothing factory. The child escaped a year later, and Sly spent a year in jail where he met Marvin Cromwell. They shared a cell. Marvin and Sly became close friends. Marvin's father was Edward Cromwell, the richest, most powerful man in Washington, D.C. in the 1980s. Sly worked for Edward immediately after he was released from jail. Mysteriously, all records of Sly's kidnapping conviction disappeared. There's no evidence that he ever kidnapped anyone. The only people who know about it are the child that he kidnapped, Marvin, and his probation officer, and we don't know that any of these people are still living, other than Cromwell."

"So how did you find this probation report?" Maddy asked.

"It was in his trash. He must have had it in his personal files and was trying to get rid of it before anyone found it. We definitely came to his office on the right day. Otherwise, this piece of paper would have been gone forever. I had to do a lot of digging to find out about this kidnapping conviction. I went to the Library of Congress and went through old newspaper archives. That's how I found Exhibit C—the one and only article that discusses his conviction. There were no other articles. It was as if someone went through the library archives and erased them all."

"And finally… Exhibit D. Pictures of all of us."

We all gasped.

"Oh my God, where did he get these? Why does he have these? I'm freaked out, J.P. What do we do?" Sofie asked.

"We need to find out how Sly got these pictures. Someone has told him about us, and we need to find out who." I responded. "He's onto us." Considering all of the evidence in front of us that showed how dangerous Sly was, I was surprised at how calm I was.

"Should we tell our parents?" I asked as I could see the tears rising in Sofie's eyes.

"They will definitely make us stop our efforts if we do," I said, feeling defeated. "Izzy, you were right. This is dangerous."

Everyone was looking up at me as if they were waiting for me to come up with the next step. Their eyes pleaded with me to tell them that everything was going to be okay. I was usually confident that I could come up with a solution to every problem, but this time, I wasn't so sure. This was a situation unlike any that I had ever dealt with before.

"Guys, I can't lie to you. I'm scared. I know that you are scared too. We have two options. One, we can stop now. Sly might still come after us, but we can stop and assure him that we are not out to threaten his job and that we will stop our fight to get kids the right to vote." Everyone was looking down at the table in deep thought.

"The second option is to continue fighting. But, if we continue fighting, we can't be afraid. We have to be courageous. Sly is going to rear his ugly head sooner or later, and when he does, we *cannot* back down. I want us to take a vote. Everyone is welcome to back out at any time, even if the team votes 'yes' now. If you feel like this is too risky, you don't have to do this. We will all still be best friends in the end. Let's vote," I announced.

"I'm in!" Izzy shouted.

"This vote is anonymous, Izzy! Please write 'yes' or 'no' on a piece of paper and pass the paper to me."

Everyone scribbled their vote on a small sheet of paper and passed their folded paper vote to me at the front of the table. I tallied the votes and then read each one individually.

"One vote for 'yes.'"

Maddy wrote down the tally on the chalkboard.

"Another vote for yes."

"A third vote for yes."

I read the final vote. "The last vote is—yes! We're all in!" I was elated. The mere thought of losing any of our team members upset me. The unanimous vote rejuvenated my spirit, and a sense of newfound courageousness came over me.

"We've got enough evidence to get Sly out of office right now. But, our cause is bigger than just Sly. We need to use this evidence to show that not only should this evil man not be elected, but that kids should have a voice in who runs their government, a government that determines what kids have to do. This evidence is great to support our argument. We will need to appeal to both the hearts and the minds of the judge who will decide if kids should be given the right to vote. This evidence will tug at their heart strings, but we need legal support too."

"Sofie, how are you coming on the legal research?"

"I've found some great cases that discuss equal rights—Fourteenth Amendment stuff that we learned about in law school." Sofie passed around copies of the cases that she had researched. "The United States Constitution says that all men are created equal. All men should mean men, women, girls, and boys, right? These cases basically say the same thing.

All people should be entitled to the same rights."

"Good job, Sofie. We'll definitely use these cases."

"Maddy, we need to know how we are looking on time. How is Sly doing in the polls? How many votes do we need to get him out?"

"Right now, the race is neck and neck, with a margin of error of about .05%."

"Maddy, what does that mean? You know math is not my strongest subject," Izzy stated.

"Basically, this is a very close race. Every vote counts. If all kids between the ages of seven years old and seventeen years old were able to vote, and if they all vote against Sly, the numbers shift drastically, and Marty will have the majority of the votes. The bottom line is that, if kids can vote, Marty will definitely win!" Maddy responded confidently.

"It's time to move to the next step. We're taking this public. We've got to get the community behind us. I'm going to make flyers tonight. I will email you guys a copy of the flyers when I'm done. Can you each print out 100 of them? The flyers will talk about why kids need the right to vote. We will pass them out to all of the kids at KLA tomorrow."

"Sounds good."

"Okay."

"Sure."

"We also need to get a petition started to show that the community supports this. We will get adults to sign the petition, saying that they are in favor of kids getting the right to vote. When we argue our case, we will need to show the judge that both kids and adults support this effort. We will knock on every door in D.C. to get adults to sign the petition," I continued.

"That sounds like a good idea, but we should not knock on doors alone," Maddy chimed in.

"That's a great point, Maddy," Sofie agreed.

"Okay. Let's go in pairs. Sofie, you and Maddy will go together, and Izzy and I will go together. Cool?" I asked.

"Cool," Sofie agreed.

It was almost 5:00, and the meeting was coming to an end. "Is everyone ready?"

They all nodded. "Just remember, ladies, keep your eyes and ears open. Sly's watching us, and we must be alert. Be careful."

Everyone nodded again. We all walked upstairs, and the girls headed out of the door. I waved goodbye, hoping that I knew just what I was getting my friends into.

CHAPTER NINE

My eyes barely stayed open during first period. I had stayed up the entire night creating fliers to pass out to our classmates at KLA. Early that morning, I emailed a copy of the flyer to the girls. The flier read: "SLY'S TIME IS UP! KIDS' RIGHT TO VOTE IS RIGHT NOW!"

I asked the girls to each print out 100 fliers to bring to school. The goal was to give out all 400 fliers by the end of the day. When lunch period arrived, I was relieved. My body desperately needed some food, or I was going to crash.

"J.P, you look like a zombie," Maddy expressed when she saw me.

"That's what happens when you stay up all night trying to think about ways to get kids the right to vote and study for a math test at the same time," I replied.

"Thanks for getting these fliers done, J.P. They look great!" Maddy said enthusiastically.

"I agree, J.P.," Sofie chimed in.

"No prob, guys. Is everyone ready for today? The game plan is to give out our fliers to everyone at KLA. Students, teachers, everyone," I instructed.

"I'll pass them around during science class next period," Maddy replied.

Sofie and Izzy nodded in agreement.

"That sounds good, Maddy. Let's meet up at our lockers after school today to get ready to pass them around in the community. We need to get as many people on board as we can," I emphasized.

*****

Throughout the day, I saw red, white, and blue fliers everywhere I looked—hanging out of backpacks, pinned inside of lockers, and in people's hands. The hallways were filled with conversations about our campaign. I couldn't walk for thirty seconds without hearing the word "vote."

"Hey, did you get a voting flyer from J.P.?"

"Did you know that J.P and her friends are trying to get kids the right to vote?"

"Kids might have the right to vote soon! Isn't that cool?"

The more I heard students talking about our campaign, the more excited I became. We were closer than we had ever been before to getting our community on board with our plan, and I couldn't have been happier. I knew that we had our fair share of people that did not believe in what we were doing, but the people who were most important were the people that we were fighting for—kids. As long as kids believed in us, that was all that we needed.

"J.P., hey, I need to ask you something!" Kyle MacFarlane chased me down the hallway as I was about to go into Ms. Nicholson's class.

"Hey, Kyle! What's up? "

Kyle was a chemistry genius. He spent hours in the KLA laboratory creating all types of chemical concoctions. Every year, he and Maddy competed against each other in the KLA science competition. Just last month, Kyle had created a solution to put inside of hot drinks to keep them hot for hours. Kyle spent so much time in the lab that I rarely got the chance to talk to him, but whenever I did, he had a million questions to ask.

"So, I've seen your fliers floating around KLA. Do you think this is really going to work? I mean, what if you don't have enough support from adults?" Kyle questioned. "What if you don't have enough support from kids? I'm not trying to burst your bubble; this is just a really hard thing to do. I hope you know what you're getting yourself into," he continued.

If he didn't mean to burst my bubble, he sure had not succeeded. I was feeling great about all of the people that had expressed their support for us. I didn't want to hear about our possible defeat.

"I can't worry about the people who don't support us, Kyle." I proceeded into Ms. Nicholson's class. As I walked, I could hear Kyle walking behind me, his lab test tubes rattling in his backpack.

"I'm sorry, J.P., I didn't mean to discourage you. I'm really excited about this. I guess I just wanted to find out if you've thought about what will happen if things don't go as you planned."

"I've definitely thought about it," I replied somberly. "The truth is, I believe that when you're fighting for what's right, nothing can go wrong." I walked into Ms. Nicholson's class, leaving Kyle in the hallway looking confused. I felt bad about being impatient with Kyle. I was tired, overwhelmed, and scared. It terrified me to think that we could possibly lose the fight to get kids the right to vote. After all, we did have huge hurdles to overcome. Not only did we need support from kids, but we also needed to argue our position in court and have a judge agree with our argument.

Ms. Nicholson's class seemed to fly by, thankfully. My attention wasn't focused there anyhow. Kyle's questions inspired me further to get out into the community to rally supporters for our cause. When the bell rung, I jumped out of my seat and ran towards Sofie's locker, where she was waiting for me.

"Hey, Sofie! Have you seen Maddy and Izzy?"

"It's only 3:55, J.P. We all agreed to meet here at 4, remember?"

"Oh, yea." I was so ready to get outside and start knocking on doors.

Four o'clock rolled around, and with it, I saw Maddy and Izzy running down the hallway to meet us.

"Are we ready?!" Izzy asked with a shriek in her voice. Her excitement was contagious. We all simultaneously shouted, "Yes!"

"Okay, Maddy and Sofie, you will be passing out fliers in the southern part of the city, right?" I asked.

They both nodded in agreement.

"Izzy, you and I will take the northern part of the city." Washington, D.C. was divided into four quadrants—Northeast, Southeast, Northwest, and Southeast. "Let's get to work."

We got on our separate metro trains to begin our journey.

****

"Next stop—Columbia Heights!" Izzy and I heard the conductor of the metro announce our stop. Columbia Heights was a neighborhood very close to my neighborhood, Petworth. It was in the northwestern quadrant of the city. We hopped off of the metro train and walked to Fourteenth Street, a street loaded with stores on each side of the street and people walking quickly to their destinations.

"Izzy, let's just hand out fliers here on the street," I suggested.

"Sounds like a plan to me," Izzy responded.

"Excuse me, ma'm." I tried to stop the first person that I encountered. She quickly walked past me.

"Hi, can I talk to you for a second, sir?" Izzy attempted to stop a man who clearly did not want to be bothered.

"This is harder than I thought, Izzy," I admitted. I was already exhausted within the first five minutes of trying to hand out fliers.

We had not managed to hand out one flier in that time. The strong gusts of cold fall wind made our task even harder. "Izzy, let's go try to knock on doors. At least we won't have to stop people as they are walking."

"Let's do it," Izzy responded.

We left the crowded Fourteenth Street, and proceeded to Spring Street, filled with homes instead of storefronts. My biggest hope was that someone would open his or her door and listen to us.

****

Meanwhile, Sofie and Maddy were busy knocking on doors near Capitol Hill in the southeastern quadrant of the city. Just steps away from the houses that they were visiting was the United States Capitol building, where all of the country's laws are made.

"I'm a little nervous about talking to these strangers," Maddy told Sofie.

"It will be fine, Maddy," Sofie softly assured her and knocked on the first door.

The door slowly opened, and Sofie's calmness dissipated gradually as it opened wider.

"Hi, may I help you?" A young, brown-haired woman with deep blue eyes opened the door with a baby in her arms.

"We, we, we, umm, well-we...." Maddy could not get the words out of her mouth.

Noticing that Maddy was having a hard time, Sofie took over. "We're here because we are trying to get 500 signatures for our petition," Sofie started.

Maddy's nervousness seemed to have vanished. She reclaimed the conversation with a renewed sense of confidence. "I'm Madeline Rosenfeld, and this is Sofia Flores-Ramirez. We attend the Kids Leaders Academy, and we are lawyers. Yes, I know it's surprising, but we're eleven-year-old lawyers. We're happy to answer any questions that you might have about that but, for now, we'd like your support for our campaign to get kids the right to vote."

The woman standing in the door seemed surprised by all that Maddy had just said. "Oh my," she stated. "So, tell me about this voting campaign."

Before Sofie had a chance to say anything, Maddy stepped in again. "My friends and I have our own law firm—the law firm of J.P. Prudence & Associates. We think that kids should have the right to vote, just as adults do.

Our goal is to get enough signatures to support a petition to get kids the right to vote. We plan on making an argument to the Federal District Court soon about kids' voting rights. If we get the right to vote, we think that enough kids will vote so that Sylvester Sullivan will be voted out of office. You *do* know that he detests kids, right?"

"I had no idea." The woman's voice was filled with shock.

"Our law firm has conducted an investigation. We have proof," Sofie confirmed.

"Oh my goodness. What type of proof?" The woman's curiosity was growing.

"We found evidence that he owns a factory which uses child labor. The children that work in the factory are not paid, and there's even one child that he kidnapped and forced to work in the factory. The child escaped, and Sullivan went to jail for kidnapping. We found out about his criminal past during our investigation."

"Give me that petition! I'm signing right away." The woman quickly grabbed the petition out of Sofie's hands and scribbled her signature. "Good luck girls, and thank you for what you are doing. You are very brave." She handed the petition back to Sofie. "It would break my heart for my child to suffer because of Sullivan." She kissed the baby that she was holding in her arms.

"Thank you so much for your support!" Sofie gushed with excitement. She was thrilled that she and Maddy had received their first signature.

"I wish you luck, girls. You're changing the future of our city."

Maddy and Sofie proudly walked away with their first signature in their hands. They were far from reaching 500 signatures, but there was no better feeling than getting the first one.

****

We had been walking down Spring Street for three hours, but we'd only received three signatures. That was one signature per hour. The hour was now past 7:00, and all of our energy had faded. We needed 500 signatures, and there was no chance that we would get those signatures today.

"Izzy, I'm tired," I admitted, exhausted from knocking on over fifty doors that night.

"I am too," Izzy responded with a sense of defeat.

"Let's call it a night." I felt horrible for stopping, but I knew that it wasn't safe to knock on doors in the dark. As we walked towards the metro station, a bright red poster attached to a traffic sign caught my eye. As I got closer to the sign, I realized that I recognized the faces that appeared on the sign. I could tell that Izzy noticed the faces too. We both screamed at the same time.

"Oh my goodness, J.P.! Those pictures are of us!" They were just like the pictures that we had found in Sly's trash, except these pictures had just been taken. I noticed that the shirt that I had on in the picture was the one that I had worn the day before.

I was so shocked that I couldn't speak. The poster in front of us had pictures of me, Sofie, Izzy, and Maddy with our eyes cut out, only appearing as large black holes, with the words, "STOP NOW, OR WE WILL SEE TO IT THAT YOU ARE STOPPED." Behind our pictures, there was a picture of a man with a black mask on, with a sinister grin plastered on his face. Izzy and I looked at each other in horror. We had to get in touch with Sofie and Maddy immediately to alert them that we were in danger.

Sofie was the only one of us who had a cell phone. Izzy and I jetted back to my house and called her from my home phone.

"Sofie! Where are you? Is Maddy with you?! Are you guys okay?"

"J.P... of course we're okay. Maddy's right here. What's wrong? Calm down," Sofie responded in her usual calm tone.

"Sofie, get to your house as soon as possible. Don't let Maddy go home alone. Get your driver to take her home. We are all in danger!" I responded. I was on the verge of tears. I was terrified that something awful was going to happen to my friends, and it would be my fault. Why had I decided to try to change the law anyways? Granddaddy had warned me that I was doing something that was risky. This was more risky than I had ever imagined.

"What do you mean by 'danger'?" Sofie asked.

"While we were knocking on doors tonight, Izzy and I found a picture of all of us posted to a street sign. The pictures were of each of us. It looks like we are being followed. The photos were taken yesterday. The scariest part about the pictures was that each of our eyes is cut out. There's a man in a mask on the pictures, who is staring at us with an evil grin. It's creepy, Sofie. Someone doesn't want us doing what we are doing, and I'm afraid."

The phone went silent.

"Sofie, are you there?" I asked.

"I'm here…. What are we … going to do…?" I could hear the sound of a faint whimper in Sofie's voice. Her unusually slow tone made it very clear to me that she was just as afraid as I was.

"Let's have an emergency firm meeting tomorrow after school. We need to come up with a plan."

"Okay," Sofie said reluctantly.

"Sofie, we can't tell our parents. They will definitely make us quit if they know that we are in danger."

"They need to know! What if something happens to us?" Sofie remarked with a voice overcome with worry.

"Please just promise me that you won't say anything to them until we have our meeting tomorrow." I pleaded with Sofie.

"Oh gosh, J.P.…."

"Please, Sofie. I'm begging you."

"Okay. I won't say anything, but we need to put our safety first."

"I know. I will see you tomorrow."

CHAPTER TEN

"Y'all are meeting today?" Granny asked curiously. "I thought y'all only met on Fridays. You gals must be very busy."

"We are, Granny," I responded. I knew I sounded distant, but I had a lot on my mind. My nerves had been on edge since the moment I saw that poster.

"Are you okay, Juris?" Granny could always tell when I wasn't myself. I think that the biggest clue for her that something was wrong was that I wasn't eating her apple pie, my favorite dessert.

"I'm fine, Granny."

"You sho'? You sho' don't seem like yo' self today."

I just nodded and walked to the door to look out for the girls to arrive. My tension turned down just a notch when I saw Maddy walking down the street. I knew that she had a million questions about the poster that we had found, but Sofie had instructed her not to say anything around her parents or my grandparents. She waited quietly with me while we waited for Sofie and Izzy to arrive.

"Do you want some pie, Maddy?" Granny shouted from the kitchen.

"No, Granny. I'm okay." I knew that Maddy's rejection of Granny's pie would make Granny suspicious.

"But this is your favorite apple pie, honey," Granny responded, seeming to take Maddy's rejection personally.

"I just ate, Granny."

"All right." Granny could tell that something was wrong.

Sofie and Izzy arrived at the same time. They walked into the house without saying hello and with their heads bent down.

"What on earth is wrong with my gals today?" Granny came out of the kitchen.

"Nothing," we responded in unison. I felt terrible for not telling Granny why were so upset, but I knew that she would be worried sick if she knew that we were in danger.

As soon as Izzy closed the door, we walked downstairs to the basement without uttering a word. As soon as we sat down, my eyes filled with tears as I blurted out, "This isn't good, guys!"

"It's okay, J.P. We just need to figure out what to do next," Sofie tried to assure me.

"Well, we are clearly being followed by someone who wants us to stop our campaign. First, we found our pictures in Sly's trash, and now we find this poster," Izzy chimed in, placing the poster that we found yesterday on the table.

"Should we call the police?" I asked, desperately hoping that my friends could come up with the answer.

"If the police become involved, our parents will find out, and we will have to stop the fight to get kids the right to vote," Izzy replied.

I knew that Izzy was right, but hearing her say the words confirmed what I already knew. If we called the police, all of our hard work would be in vain because our parents would believe that our safety was at risk.

"We know that Sly is dangerous. Izzy has already discovered that he kidnapped a kid many years ago. He is capable of hurting us. He now has a reason to hurt us," Sofie asserted.

Sofie's words felt like thorns piercing my whole body. She was just being realistic, but I did not want to face the reality that Sly was on to us, and he had a motive and the means to stop us dead in our tracks.

Speaking with all of the conviction that I could muster, I stood up and placed my fist firmly on the table. "Just as I told you at our last meeting, we know that this is risky. Changing the law is dangerous work. We are facing a powerful person who knows powerful people. I can't deny the fact that we could get hurt doing what we are doing. I can't deny that I'm afraid. To tell you the truth, I have never been more afraid of something in my entire life. But guess what? I'm not stopping. I will do this alone if I have to, but I'm not stopping."

The tension in the room was palpable. I could touch, taste, and feel it. Maybe I had said too much, but I meant every word. I was dedicated to this mission, and I would not let bullies like Sly scare me out of it.

"I'm still in, J.P.," Sofie confidently asserted.

"So are we," Izzy and Maddy joined.

"You guys are the best. Thank you," I expressed with extreme gratitude.

"We have to be smart about how we move forward."

"I agree," Sofie responded.

"First, if we go out, we have to go in groups. We need one person to have a cell phone on them at all times. Sofie, you have a cell phone, so that means that either Izzy, Maddy, or I have to get one."

"I have fifty dollars saved up from my allowance," Maddy offered.

"I have thirty dollars saved up. I don't have to go shopping this weekend like I planned," Izzy generously stated. I knew that Izzy's offer was extremely kind because Izzy's favorite thing in life was to go shopping. She was saving up for a winter coat that cost seventy-five dollars, and giving us all of her savings would deplete her coat fund.

"Are you guys sure?" I asked.

"Of course, J.P."

"Well, I have twenty dollars saved. I know that's not a lot, but Granny and Granddaddy haven't been able to give me an allowance for a while." My dad had stopped sending Granny and Granddaddy money to help with my school expenses. Granny and Granddaddy had been scraping for money for the past few months. I was embarrassed to tell my friends that I couldn't afford to support our project.

"That's okay, J.P." Izzy assured me. "With all of our allowances combined, we have enough money to pay for at least one month's cell phone bill."

"Thanks, Izzy." I loved my friends because they never made me feel ashamed about how much I had or didn't have.

"We can get a cell phone after school tomorrow," Maddy continued. "So, once we have the cell phone, we need to make sure that it is on us at all times and that if we are ever facing danger, we immediately call the police."

"Got it!" Sofie agreed.

"In the meantime, we need more signatures. We are going to be taking this campaign to court soon. We will be making a legal argument. In our argument, we need to be able to say that at least 500 people support giving kids in D.C. the right to vote. We can't say that if we don't have the signatures." Maddy impressed the importance of getting the necessary number of signatures.

"Sofie, do you think that, during KLA Day, we can ask all of the students to go out and get at least two signatures for the petition?" I asked.

"That's a great idea, J.P.! There are 250 students at KLA. If each student gets two signatures, we will easily get five hundred signatures. We've already collected forty-five signatures from community members and KLA students. We don't have that many more to get, just 455 more," Maddy stated.

We were all waiting on Sofie's answer about asking the student body to help us collect signatures. After all, she was the class president, and she would be the person asking the student body for signatures. Collecting 455 more signatures before arguing our case in court sounded overwhelming. It was critical that we got help collecting the signatures if we were really going to get this done.

"I just want to make sure that we don't put anyone at risk. Putting ourselves at risk is one thing, but I'm not sure how comfortable I feel about asking our classmates to put themselves at risk," Sofie reasoned.

Sofie took her responsibilities as class president seriously; I knew that she would need more time to reflect on this. "I also don't want to get Sly even angrier. When he sees that we have 250 people on the streets trying to get kids the right to vote, he will go berserk. I don't want him going berserk on us," Sofie reasoned. I could tell that she was talking herself through my proposal to her.

"You don't have to make a decision now, Sofie. Take your time. I know that this is a big decision," I said understandingly.

"Let me take some time and think about this. KLA Day is a week away, so I will let you know as soon as I make a decision. Okay?"

"Okay." I wanted a decision soon, but I had to respect Sofie's role as student council president and her obligation to put the best interests of the student body first. "Even though we don't have all of the signatures that we need, we still have to get started on writing our legal brief that we will argue before the Federal District Court for the District of Columbia. We need to get the petition signed, but it's also important that we get our brief written."

A brief is a written argument that a judge reads when he or she is making a decision about a case. I was thinking ahead. We had three weeks until the election, and the judge would have to hear our case in order to get the law changed. This judge had to make the ultimate decision to change the law.

"I have almost finished all of the research that we will need to write the brief," Sofie informed me.

"Great!" I replied. I was relieved. I felt like our firm had faced so many challenges—the lack of sufficient signatures for the petition, the threatening posters, the time crunch of the pending election—I wanted to feel like we were making some progress.

"I'll ask my dads if we can have a sleepover at my house on Friday. We can have a brief writing party! If we start writing after school, it will be hard, but we can finish the brief by Saturday morning. What do you think?"

"That sounds like so much fun, Izzy!" Maddy beamed with excitement. We all loved sleepovers at Izzy's house.

"Yes! That would be great, Izzy." I shared Maddy's enthusiasm.

"Okay, I will ask my dads tonight, and I will let you guys know tomorrow," Izzy stated.

It was almost 5:00, and everyone had to get home. "I think it's time to wrap up, guys. I'm so glad that we met today. We're back on track. Let's do this!" As we were packing up our stuff, the phone rang. "I'll get it, Granny! I yelled upstairs. Granddaddy had put a phone in the basement so that our firm could make phone calls.

"Hello…?" I answered.

"Good evening, Juris." The ominous voice on the other end of the phone greeted me.

"Umm…. Who is this?" I asked timidly.

"You will find out soon enough, Juris." The person hung up abruptly.

"J.P., who was that?" Sofie asked. The girls could tell that something had unnerved me.

"I have no idea, but I think that it was Sly. We have an enemy, and he's onto us."

CHAPTER ELEVEN

KLA Day was my favorite day of the year, except for my birthday and Christmas. Walking into KLA today, students could not help but feel overwhelmed with school pride. The hallways were flooded in a sea of blue and orange; balloons, posters, and students wearing blue and orange t-shirts and hats filled the hallways. Each year, students raised money to help a local charity in the city.

Every KLA Day, I sold Granny's pies during the KLA Day bake sale and donated all of the proceeds to charity. My classmates at KLA had been asking me for weeks whether Granny was planning to make her pies this year, and I had promised them that she would. Over the last few weeks, I had created a five-page list of students who had put in a special order for Granny's pie. They made me promise that I would sell them a piece before opening up the sale of the pie to the rest of the student body.

Our school-wide pep rally was later this afternoon, after fifth period. Sofie had not yet decided whether she would get the KLA student body involved with knocking on doors to support the campaign to get kids the right to vote. I knew that making that request to our classmates would be a big deal for her, and I did not want to pressure her into making any decisions. As student council president, I wanted her to feel completely comfortable presenting such a dangerous task to the KLA students.

Before getting to the pep rally, I first had to get through Ms. Nicholson's class. Despite how much Nitpick Nicholson got under my skin, over these last few weeks, I realized that her history class was actually my favorite class. I never knew how much our country's history affected the present day until my friends and I started our voting rights campaign for kids.

"Students, today is KLA Day, as you know," Nitpick Nicholson began. "I know that you tend to get a little anxious, and your attention is easily diverted on KLA Day, but it would behoove you to pay close attention to our lesson today. We have a test next week on the Voting Rights Act of 1965, and everything that we discuss today will be on your test."

I wasn't too worried about this test. After all, I had been working on voting rights in my free time for the past several weeks. I knew all that there was to know about the Voting Rights Act.

Ms. Nicholson's class proceeded without a hitch. After her class, I was confident that I would get an "A" on my test. There was nothing that she discussed that I didn't already know. The bell rang before I knew it, and I went to my locker to drop off my history book and pick up my books for the rest of my classes. After my math, science, art, and English classes, the last bell finally rung, and I was off to the auditorium to sell Granny's pies and to get ready for our school pep rally.

A table was waiting for me to set up Granny's pies for the bake sale. As soon as I put the last pie on the table, I looked up and saw a long line filled with students. "J.P., I'd like four slices of pie. I'm taking some home for my parents," Kennedy Singleton announced. Kennedy was a student in our KLA law program, and she had been buying Granny's pies each KLA Day since our first one. As the bake sale got underway, my supply of pies quickly dwindled. I sadly had to tell Kyle MacFarlane that we had sold the last pie when he got to the front of the line.

Wrapping up the bake sale, I counted the money that we had earned and realized that Granny's pies had made over 500 dollars. This was the most money that I had ever earned from selling pies at KLA Day! I couldn't wait to share the news with Sofie. Our class was sure to win the KLA Day contest with this much money. The best part was that all of the money was going towards a great cause.

Sofie walked into our school auditorium, proudly donning her KLA colors. Sofie had been our class president for four years. During each KLA Day school event, Sofie wore a large circular pin that read, "KLA School President." Every time I saw her wearing her president's pin, I was taken aback with pride. Sofie was generally a shy person, but when she stepped into her role as president, her whole personality changed. It was as if a newfound sense of confidence came over her.

I walked over to her where she was standing with the rest of our school's elected officers. "Hey, Sofie! I know that the pep rally is about to start, but I just wanted to let you know that the pies made $500! I think our class is going to win the contest!"

"Fantastic, J.P.," Sofie responded quickly, seeming a bit preoccupied. I could tell that Sofie was mentally preparing herself to speak in front of our class. I decided to leave her alone so that she could collect her thoughts. "Okay, Sofie. I'm going to find Maddy and Izzy. Break a leg out there!"

"Thanks, J.P.!" Sofie said, barely looking up from the pad of paper where she had written down the speech that she planned to give to our class. I couldn't help but wonder if she had made a decision about getting our class to help with the voting petition.

"J.P.!" I heard Maddy call my name. Maddy didn't like our school pep rallies because she did not feel comfortable being in large crowds, much preferring to be in smaller groups. I ran over to her, knowing that she was getting antsy by the growing crowd of students pouring into the auditorium.

"Hey Maddy, let's wait outside for Izzy." Before every pep rally, we all gathered in our usual spot by the snack machine. As we waited for Izzy, we could hear the cadence of the KLA marching band drums echoing throughout the auditorium, triggering cheers and shouts from our energetic classmates, each yelling out their class year. "Where is Izzy?" I was getting impatient. One of my favorite parts of KLA Day was hearing the marching band play our KLA school song.

After waiting for what seemed like a decade, Izzy finally strolled over to us. Izzy was wearing a bright blue and orange dress that she had designed and sewn together herself. The blue bottom of the dress was pleated and flowed out, like a 1950s vintage skirt. Izzy's orange top had the letters KLA sprinkled all over it. It looked like she had been working on the dress for months now. Izzy was meticulous about the clothes that she created.

"Let's go, Izzy. The pep rally is about to start." I hurried my friends into the auditorium, maneuvering through the students standing on the floor so that we could get a seat close to the band and our school officers. I wanted to sit as close as possible to Sofie when she was giving her speech.

As soon as we took our seats, the KLA band began playing our school song. I knew that Sofie would be making her speech immediately after they finished playing. As we finished singing my favorite verse from our school song, Sofie walked onto the stage with the rest of our class officers, singing the final verse on her microphone. "KLA, we learn in your way/KLA, where all is right and true. KLA, we'll never stray/we will forever adorn your orange and blue...."

"Good afternoon, KLA classmates. My name is Sofia Flores-Ramirez, and I have been proud to serve as your class president for the past four years." The audience busted out in clapping and cheers. "There are several things that we as KLA students have to be proud of this year. One thing that I am particularly proud of today is the fact that we have raised over $2,000 to benefit homeless shelters in D.C. We have counted the money raised from all classes, and the winner of this year's fundraising contest goes to ... the sixth grade class! You will have the honor of pie-ing our principal at the end of this pep rally! And-next month, you will all visit the White House!"

When my class was announced as the winner, the sixth grade section of the auditorium erupted into clapping and shouting. I was so happy that we won, and even happier that Granny's pies had helped us do it. The clapping faded away, and Sofie continued her speech.

"We continue to serve our community and help those who are less fortunate than us. We are leaders, and I am proud to call you my classmates, but more importantly, I am glad to call you my friends." Sofie paused.

"Over the past several weeks, you may have been approached by me, J.P. Prudence, Maddy Rosenfeld, or Izzy Carrington. We have likely asked you for your support in helping us get kids the right to vote. Over these weeks, we have been working night and day to accomplish this goal. I have struggled with this decision, but I must ask you now...." At that moment, I knew that Sofie had made the decision. Tears welled up in my eyes as she continued her speech.

"We need your help. The right to vote for kids is an idea that is new, and one that the law has never recognized. We are fighting a huge battle, and we need the support of our community behind us. I ask that you go out into your neighborhoods, knock on doors, and ask your neighbors to sign our petition to get kids the right to vote." You could hear a pin drop in the auditorium. Everyone was glued to what Sofie was saying.

"Next week, we will be arguing our case to get kids the right to vote in front of the Federal District Court for the District of Columbia. To change the law, we need to have a petition signed by at least 500 people, and we need the judge to take our side during our argument. My friends and I are working on the legal argument to present to the judge, but we desperately need your help getting 500 signatures. We have only collected 45.

"In three days, we will give our written argument to the court. We can't submit this argument until the signatures are collected. This weekend, while we finish writing our brief, I need you knocking on every single door that you can to get support for this mission.

"I must tell you that this won't be easy. People will laugh at you. They will stare at you like you're crazy when you tell them that you are trying to get kids the right to vote. Don't be discouraged.

"I also must also tell you that there is some danger involved with this. There are people who do not want kids to get the right to vote. Sylvester Sullivan is one of those people. You must be careful if you decide to accept my request. I do not want you to put yourself in danger or feel that you have to do this, so if you feel that this is too dangerous, remember you do not have to do this.

"But, if you do this, remember, you are a part of a movement, a movement that started with us, but will affect our children, our grandchildren, and their children.

"We are reaching for the stars with this campaign. We will not stop until we reach those stars, and those stars are the right for kids to vote. Can I count on your promise to help us?"

The student body started clapping and faint "yeses" reverberated throughout the auditorium.

"I can't hear you! Can I count on you?!" Sofie said with a sense of fervor that I had never before witnessed in her. The faint "yeses" turned into confident and clear "YESES!" from my classmates.

"ONE MORE TIME—CAN I COUNT ON YOU, KLA?!" Sofie shouted in the loudest voice that I had ever heard come out of her usually soft-spoken mouth.

This time, the entire KLA student body shouted in unison, "YES!" Applause poured throughout the audience as Sofie walked off of the stage. The band replayed our KLA song and our classmates sang with renewed school spirit. As the band continued to play, I walked over to Sofie who looked exhausted but relieved.

"Sofie, you're the best!" I hugged my best friend.

"This is bigger than us, J.P. We are fighting for generations to come. It's the least I could do," Sofie responded.

We joined in our school song, the perfect ending to the best KLA Day that I had ever seen.

CHAPTER TWELVE

It had been a long week, and I couldn't wait to get to Izzy's house. I loved talking to her dads. I always wished that I saw my dad more often than just during the holidays, but Izzy's dads gave me an idea of what it was like to have a father that was around every day. One reason that I think Izzy and I were best friends is because we both understood what it was like to miss our biological parents.

When I walked into Izzy's building, I checked in with her doorman. Izzy came downstairs minutes after the doorman alerted her that I was there. Izzy escorted me to her condominium unit. Izzy lived in the coolest building in the northeast quadrant of D.C. There was a swimming pool on the roof of her building. During the summers, we always had the best pool parties at her house. Her actual condominium unit was surrounded by glass, and she lived on one of the highest floors in the building. When you looked outside of her bedroom, you could see the United States Capitol.

"How is my favorite Juris Prudence?" When I walked into Izzy's house, Scott Carrington was sitting in his usual lounge chair watching the evening news. Every time he saw me, Scott called me his "favorite Juris Prudence." It always made me laugh.

"I'm doing well. Thanks for letting us stay over tonight."

"Of course! We have pizzas coming soon, and Jeff made brownies for you guys last night. I know that they aren't as good as your grandmother's, but he tried. Just try to act like you like them."

I giggled again.

"Are Sofie and Maddy on their way? I asked, trying to hide my worry. Since the strange phone call, seeing our pictures posted in Columbia Heights, and learning about Sly's criminal past, I found myself in a constant state of worry about my friends and myself. I knew that Sly would do anything that he needed to do to stop us, even if that meant hurting us. When my friends were not in my immediate presence, I was restless until I knew that they were safe.

"Yep—I talked to them a few minutes ago," Izzy responded nonchalantly. Maddy and Sofie had gone to pick up our firm's new cell phone after school. "What time did they say that they would be here?" I inquired further.

"J.P., chill out. They will be here soon." Izzy always became very short when she was frustrated. She didn't seem to care that Sly was an ex-convict who was stalking us.

The door buzzed, and Scott went to answer it. Sofie and Maddy were standing in the doorway. I'd never felt more relieved in my life until I saw my best friends standing at the door, safe and sound.

"Hello ladies!" Scott greeted Sofie and Maddy. "Come in. You got here just in time. Isabelle just ordered pizza."

"Great, I'm starving!" Maddy replied. When Maddy was hungry, she didn't care about anything other than eating. She failed to mention the firm's new cell phone.

"Did you guys get the phone?" I asked impatiently.

"Yes, J.P. Here it is." Sofie pulled our new cell phone out of her bag.

I was thrilled to see our shiny, new phone. We now had everything that we needed to make our firm a real, functioning law firm. More importantly, we had everything that we needed to stay safe while we were out promoting our campaign to get kids the right to vote.

Our pizza arrived, and over dinner, we updated Scott on all that we had been doing for the campaign. We didn't mention the threats that we had received, because we didn't want Scott to worry and make us stop. "You girls have been very busy. Just be careful out there. I'm sure that there are some people that don't want you to be successful with this mission," Scott commented.

We all looked down at the table in silence. Scott's words struck a chord with all of us. To break the awkward silence, I quickly changed the subject. "Are we ready to start writing our brief? We have to file this thing in court on Monday, and it's already Friday."

"I'm ready," Sofie chimed in. Izzy nodded in agreement.

"I have to finish my pizza first. Then I'll be ready." Maddy seemed annoyed by my impatience to begin writing before she was done eating. We let Maddy finish her pizza, and we thanked Scott again for allowing us to stay over.

"Any time girls," Scott welcomed us. "Good luck writing this brief tonight. Don't work too hard."

We graduated from the kitchen table and into Izzy's room. Izzy's room was like an art museum. Her room, like the rest of the house, was surrounded by glass, allowing us to see the spectacular sites of Washington, D.C. My favorite site to view from Izzy's room was the Washington Monument, the tallest structure in the District of Columbia. Izzy's room was covered with Izzy's artwork, ranging from Korean-inspired sculptures to paintings of different places in the District of Columbia. Every time that I visited Izzy, she had added a new piece of art to her wall. The borders of Izzy's room were lined with brightly colored beanbag chairs. We all took a seat in a different beanbag chair.

"Okay, let's split up the work. Izzy, you write the introduction. Sofie and Maddy, you write the body, and I will write the conclusion." I directed. We each had laptop computers from school, and we wasted no time getting to work. Each of us began typing frantically, trying to finish our brief before the morning. The floor of Izzy's room quickly flooded with paper. Over the course of the last few weeks, we had collected mounds of cases, evidence about Sly, newspaper articles, and other information that we planned to discuss in our brief. Izzy's bright pink rug was now a sea of white papers.

Even though we were working, like at all of our sleepovers, we couldn't help ourselves from talking nonstop. After hours of working, the time was 2:00 in the morning., and we were getting sleepier and sillier. "Sofie, why did the squirrel fall out of the tree?" I asked.

"I don't know!" Sofie giggled.

"Because it was sleeping!" I couldn't stop laughing. The other girls just looked at me confused.

We continued to laugh and joke while writing our brief. Izzy, who usually asked random questions, did not let the opportunity pass to present a question to the group.

"Chicas, question—what's one thing that someone in this room has that you wish you have, but you don't? Maddy, you go first."

"Hmmm…. That's a hard question. Let me think for a few minutes." Maddy quietly reflected while we waited for her to answer. "J.P., I wish I had your bravery. You are not afraid of anything."

"That's so nice of you, Maddy." I was touched by Maddy's words. "You're brave in more ways than you know. You're the only person I know who can recreate volcanic eruptions and doesn't flinch when doing it."

"Sofie, you're next. What do you wish you had that one of us has?" Izzy repeated her question.

"Well, I'm really jealous of the amount of time that you guys are able to spend with your families. J.P. can always talk to her grandmother and grandfather about her day. And Izzy, you and your dads do such fun stuff after school and on the weekends. So do you, Maddy. I don't have any of that. My parents are always working. I only see Maria and Gabriel. I miss my parents."

I hugged Sofie. "We are your family too, Sofie."

"I know, but there's nothing like having your mom and dad around."

"You know I know that more than anyone," I responded. "I guess I'll go next. I want parents like you guys have. I've never met my mom, and no one in my house talks about her. I only see my dad a few times a year. He's too busy trying to chase his acting career in New York. He doesn't even call me on my birthday. You guys have parents that you live with and know. I will never have that." I could feel the tears rising in my eyes, while a lump grew in my throat. I didn't want to cry. Yet, whenever I thought about my biological parents, I couldn't help but feel like I was missing out on a huge part of my life.

"Oh, don't cry, J.P." Izzy tried to comfort me. "This question wasn't meant to make everyone sad. I was just curious. I will go next."

"I can definitely understand missing your biological parents. My dads adopted me from Korea. I've never even seen pictures of my biological parents. There's no way that I will ever know where I came from. I love my dads, but whenever we all go out, I get weird stares. Most people have a mom and a dad, but I have a non-traditional family. I get tired of explaining my family to people. My dads aren't even the same color as me, so no one believes that I am their daughter until I tell them that my dads adopted me. One day, I want to walk into a place, tell someone that I have two dads, and I want that person to just say, 'okay,' without questioning me and making me feel like an outcast."

I could tell that this was something that had been on Izzy's mind for a while.

"You guys don't have to provide an explanation when you tell someone that you are related to your parents or your grandparents, J.P.," Izzy continued.

Hearing my friends talk about what they covet gave me a perspective about them that I'd never had before. On the outside, it seemed like my friends had it all. Tonight, I realized that we were all missing something that we would give anything to have, but was beyond our control and ability to possess.

We continued writing the brief, tired from the hours growing later, and somewhat heavy-hearted from the conversation that we had just had. As the clock approached three o'clock in the morning, we slowly drifted off into dreamland, first Sofie, then Izzy, then Maddy and then me.

****

The bright orange sun rose over the Capitol building and burst into the glass of Izzy's bedroom, alerting us that morning had officially arrived. We each gradually woke up, noticing that we had fallen asleep in our clothes and on top of our documents.

"How are we coming on the brief, team?" I had completed my part, but I didn't know how far the other girls had gotten. I was afraid that we had loads of work to do before the brief would be done.

"I'm done," Maddy mumbled, still waking up from her sleep.

"So are we," Izzy and Sofie stated drowsily.

"Awesome!" I shouted in relief. Our brief was done, and I knew that we were almost to the finish line. Now, all we had to do was proofread our work and take it to the courthouse to file it with the courthouse clerk. "Chicas, this has been the best sleepover ever. You guys are the best friends that a girl could ask for," I remarked.

We printed out our different portions of the brief. I was going to review the whole thing and make any corrections that needed to be made before I took it to the courthouse on Monday.

It was Saturday, and we all had family obligations to attend to that day. Maddy's brother's bar mitzvah was quickly approaching, and she had to get back home to help her family make arrangements for the big day. Sofie and Izzy were doing chores around their houses, and I had to help Granny and Granddaddy prepare for a yard sale at their senior citizens club. As we discussed how excited we were that the brief was finished, we packed our belongings. We all thanked Scott for letting us sleep over and told him to give our thanks to Jeff, Izzy's other dad, who was out of town for the weekend.

I said goodbye to my friends, more thankful than ever for their friendship. Our talk the night before made me realize that, although we all felt that we were missing something in our lives, we were all incredibly fortunate to have something priceless, and that something was each other.

****

I left Izzy's house, and walked towards my bike to begin my ride home. As I got closer to my bike, I could not help but notice a black figure in my peripheral vision. Carrying our finished brief in my briefcase made me feel like I was carrying eggshells. I was so afraid of anything happening to the brief or it getting into the wrong hands before we had a chance to file it in court. The ominous black figure that I noticed did not relieve my sense of anxiety. The figure disappeared every time I turned around, but I could not shake the feeling that this black figure was following me.

By the time that I reached my bike, the black figure had vanished, and I was relieved. I mounted my bike as fast as I could, and sped home. When the door to my house was in my immediate eyesight, I peddled even faster, wanting to get inside as soon as possible. Despite how much I wanted to believe that the sense of danger that I felt walking to my bike and riding home was a figment of my imagination, something deep down inside of me knew that the danger was real.

"Good morning, Juris!" Granny welcomed me as I walked into the house. "You done writing your brief?" Granny's voice carried a sense of comfort that always calmed me down when I was feeling nervous. Walking into the house, she immediately made me feel like all was good and peaceful in the world, just by the sound of her voice.

"Yes, ma'am!" I answered sheepishly, still tired from staying up so late. "We stayed up almost all night to finish it." I reached down into my briefcase to show Granny the finished product. As I reached, I noticed a large hole in my briefcase. It appeared as though someone had used a knife to slice the briefcase open. I gasped in shock.

"What's wrong, Juris? How did you tear your briefcase, honey?"

"I'm not really sure, Granny. I'm so sorry." I felt terrible knowing that my mother's most prized possession had been damaged. Not wanting Granny to worry, I tried to mask the realization that someone had tried to rob me this morning on my way back home. I frantically searched for the brief, desperately hoping that the person who had cut my briefcase had not taken it. Before leaving Izzy's house, I had put the brief inside of a folder, and zipped it into a hidden compartment in my briefcase. Luckily, the culprit had not managed to get to it, and it was exactly where I had put it when leaving Izzy's. The hole in my briefcase confirmed that the black figure that I'd noticed was not something that I had simply imagined. Someone was really after me, and I knew exactly who it was.

Not wanting to show that I was preoccupied, I focused my attention on the brief. "Granny, can you proofread our brief tonight after the seniors' yard sale?"

"Of course, Juris. I can't wait to read it. I already know that you gals did a fantastic job writing it. I wouldn't expect any less of you." Granny's words of encouragement put me at ease. Once she read over our brief, I knew that we would be ready to take the brief to the courthouse.

This morning, Granny, Granddaddy, and I were preparing to volunteer at our neighborhood yard sale. All of the proceeds were going to help homeless people in Washington, D.C. Granny had baked an apple pie for the event. Still warm from the oven, I grabbed the pie, which was cooling off on the kitchen counter. We loaded all of our unwanted furniture and clothes into our neighbor's car, since no one in my house drove, and rode off to the yard sale, which was being held at our neighborhood recreation center.

When we arrived at the center, Granny and Granddaddy's friends greeted us. "Hello, Prudence Family!" Ms. Geraldine Johnson exclaimed. "And my precious, Juris. You have gotten so tall, honey. How have you been? I hear that you are out here being a wonderful lawyer. I heard all about your new law firm. We are all so proud of you, darling." Ms. Johnson was one of my favorite people. Whenever I saw her, she always expressed so much interest in my activities as a lawyer. Today, I was elated to know that she was interested in our firm's campaign to get kids the right to vote.

During the yard sale, several of the volunteers and customers came up to me to discuss the campaign. As I helped sell our old belongings, I discussed why it was important for kids to get the right to vote. All that our law firm had done so far to change the law intrigued the yard sale customers and volunteers. The conversations that I had with people at the yard sale affirmed what had not been so apparent to me before—people were genuinely interested in helping us change the law. I left the yard sale feeling encouraged by the supporters that I had met there.

****

When we arrived back at home, Granny sat down at the living room table with a cup of coffee and put on her reading glasses. She had a red ink pen in her hand. Whenever she read one of my papers, she was meticulous about making sure that there were no mistakes in the paper. Tonight, while reading the brief, I knew that she would be equally diligent about ensuring that the final brief that we gave to the court on Monday would be perfect. Granny did not like being bothered while she was reading, so I left her alone at the table to edit the brief. I knew that, in the morning, I would find our brief covered in red ink.

That day had shown me that while there were definitely people in the city that were trying hard to stop me and my friends from continuing our fight to change the law, there were also people that genuinely cared about our efforts and wanted us to succeed. Those were the people that mattered, and those were the people that I was determined to make proud.

CHAPTER THIRTEEN

When Monday morning rolled around, I woke up exhausted. I had spent all day Sunday making the changes that Granny suggested for our brief. On Sunday evening, I finalized the brief, printed it out on fresh white paper, put it into a shiny black folder, with a label that read, "Submitted by the Law Firm of Juris P. Prudence & Associates," and placed the folder in my briefcase.

I could barely sleep the night before. I knew that I had to race the brief to the courthouse before school, and I did not want to face any problems on the way there. That morning, I got ready for school, throwing on the first thing that I saw in my closet. After snapping on my helmet and securing my briefcase on my bike rack, I ferociously peddled to the courthouse. I got to the United States District Court for the District of Columbia the moment that the courthouse doors opened. After locking up my bike, I ran inside of the courthouse. As I went through the courthouse security line, the security guard suspiciously observed me. "What's a young lady like yourself doing here this morning on a school day?" he cautiously asked.

"I'm an attorney," I answered proudly.

He looked puzzled. "Say what?"

"I'm an attorney, and I'm filing a brief today," I repeated. "Can you please direct me to the clerk's office?" I asked courteously. The clerk's office in a courthouse is the place where lawyers submit legal briefs.

"Young lady, the clerk's office is down the hall, first door to the right, but I hope that you know that it's illegal to lie about being an attorney." The guard did not believe that I was a lawyer.

"Yes, sir. I understand that." I thanked the guard for his directions to the clerk's office and walked quickly in the direction to which he had guided me, holding my briefcase tightly.

I walked into the clerk's office, relieved that I had finally made it. Carefully, I took the brief out of my briefcase, not wanting to bend the edges of the folder that protected the brief. "Good morning, honey." The clerk greeted me.

"Hi." I was too excited to say anything else, and I quickly handed the folder over to the clerk. My pride was bursting at the seams as I delivered the product that our firm had worked so hard to create.

"What's this that you have here for me?" the clerk asked, full of curiosity.

"It's my law firm's brief. We would like to file it with the court."

"A law firm? You don't say. Good for you, sweetie," the clerk said. "I'll take your brief. Good luck." I confidently signed over the brief to the clerk and walked out of the courthouse, feeling more confident than ever that we were well on our way to getting kids the right to vote. All we had to do now was argue our position in front of the judge, and hopefully, the judge would rule that kids could vote. If kids voted, they would most certainly vote Sly out of office.

With these positive thoughts inundating my head, I went to retrieve my bike from the bike rack where I had locked it. When I went over to unlock my bike, my heart sunk. My bike was missing. In its place was a note that read, "I warned you to stop. Keep going, and your bike will not be the only thing missing."

Immediately, I knew who was responsible for taking one of my most prized possessions.

My bike had special value to me. My grandparents had saved up for months to buy my bike because I had been asking for a bike for a whole year. Granddaddy worked a second job to make sure that he and Granny could get that bike for my birthday. They would be devastated when I told them that it had been stolen. They would be even more distraught when I told them that Sly had stolen the bike, and I *had* to tell them. I was tired of hiding the fact that my friends and I were in danger.

Knowing that I would be late to school that morning, I sadly walked to the metro station, heading back to my neighborhood. I had to tell Granny and Granddaddy the whole truth and nothing but the truth.

****

Granny and Granddaddy were shocked when they heard my key opening the front door.

"What in the world are you doing here, Juris?" Granny questioned.

"Hi, Granny." My throat started hurting as I choked up. "Gra … gra … granny…" I couldn't hold back my tears.

"Sylvester Sullivan is following me and my friends. He's a dangerous man, and he wants to hurt us. He cut a hole in my briefcase, and he stole my bike this morning at the courthouse." I poured all of this out to Granny in one breath. After I got my last word out, my tears flowed uncontrollably.

Granny embraced me with her arms. "Slow down, honey, and tell Granny what's going on."

After collecting myself, I slowed down and clearly explained the threats that we had been receiving from Sly and why my bike was missing.

"We must call the police, Juris," Granny responded. "I'm concerned about you gals. This Sly fellow is dangerous, and I don't want him doin' anything to hurt you or my gals." Granny's immense concern was evident. I was terrified that she would make me stop working on our project. We had come so far, and despite all of the threats, I did not want to stop now.

"I'm happy that your brief got filed, Juris. All you need to do next is make your argument in court. We will patch up Ann's briefcase, and we will let the police handle Sullivan." Granddaddy calmly piped in.

I was elated that Granny and Granddaddy weren't making me stop the campaign to get kids the right to vote. After all, my friends, my classmates, and my community were counting on my law firm.

Granny reported the threats and my missing bike to the police and told me not to worry. A police officer came to my house to question me about the threats that my friends and I had been receiving. I showed the officer the evidence that we had pulled from Sly's trash and the other threatening notes that we had received. The police officer let me and my grandparents know that they would be investigating Sly. There was something deep down inside of me, however, that wouldn't let me relinquish the feeling that even the police couldn't stop Sly.

When the police officer left, Granny continued to comfort me. "Juris, I want you to focus on preparing for your argument this week. Don't let anything distract you from winning. You and your friends have worked too hard to be defeated now by this nonsense."

With Granny's word of encouragement, I collected my belongings and went to school. I had one thing to do this week, and that was prepare for the biggest legal argument that I would probably ever make in my life.

CHAPTER FOURTEEN

Each night for the rest of the week, I spent hours rehearsing the argument that I would soon be making before the Federal District Court for the District of Columbia. Friday would be here before I knew it. With each day that passed, my anticipation heightened. On Wednesday night, less than two days before my argument in court, Granny and Granddaddy set up a mock courtroom in our living room. They pretended to be judges as I made the argument to get kids the right to vote.

"These are the reasons why kids should have the right to vote, Your Honor." I concluded my mock argument before my grandparents.

"Thank you, Miss Prudence. I have a question for you." Granddaddy pretended to be a judge, using the most serious voice that he could muster. I couldn't help but chuckle a little. "Are kids smart enough to vote?" Granddaddy continued.

"That's a great question, Your Honor." I paused. I had not thought about this question. I had always just assumed that kids were smart. "Just because we're not adults, doesn't mean that we are not smart. Some of the greatest historical figures have been kids. Anne Frank wrote a diary at the age of thirteen years old, which changed the world after it was published. Kids change the world every day. So to answer your question, yes, kids are smart enough to vote," I asserted confidently.

Granddaddy nodded. "Very good, Miss Prudence. The court will take these arguments under consideration. Court adjourned." Granddaddy banged his mock gavel, and we all started laughing. "Juris, you're soundin' good, baby girl," Granddaddy assured me. "The judge will certainly have a lot to think about on Friday after you make your argument. No matter what happens, I'm very proud of you and your friends."

With Granddaddy's vote of confidence, I wrapped up my practice for the night and got ready for bed. In less than forty-eight hours, my friends and I would potentially change history.

****

Thursday was a blur to me. All day, people were approaching me, Izzy, Maddy, and Sofie, giving us words of encouragement, and letting us know that they would be coming out to the courthouse to support us the following day. Our KLA principal had given all students permission to go to the courthouse to watch our argument, even though it was to take place on a school day. Knowing that the entire school would be watching me make this argument added to the pressure that I already felt. What if I messed up? What if I couldn't remember what to say? What if the judge asked questions that I couldn't answer? By the end of the day, my stomach was filled with knots.

My school day ended with an announcement over the loudspeakers by our principal, Mr. Marshall. "Let's thank Juris P. Prudence, Sofia Flores-Ramirez, Isabelle Carrington, and Madeline Rosenfeld when we see them. These girls represent the law firm of Juris P. Prudence & Associates, and I'd like to let them know that KLA is very proud of the work that they have done to try to get kids the right to vote. KLA students, I remind you that you must be seated in the courthouse tomorrow by 8:00 in the morning. I will see everyone at the courthouse in the morning." After Mr. Marshall's announcement, the final bell rung, and I ran to the metro station. I didn't want to waste any time. I wanted to go home and practice my argument until tomorrow morning. Game time would be here before I knew it.

****

Game time had arrived. Granny woke me up at 6:00 A.M. "Juris, good mornin', honey," Granny said calmly, sitting by my bedside. "Today is your big day."

"Good morning, Granny." I responded, a bit disoriented. "Today's the day?" I couldn't believe that I'd be in front of a judge in a couple of hours.

"Yes, honey. It's time to get ready. Your grandfather and I bought you a new black suit. It's hanging up in your closet."

"Thank you so much, Granny. You and Granddaddy didn't have to do that," I said. I knew that Granny and Granddaddy didn't have extra money to spend on my clothes.

"Of course we did. It's not every day that our baby gets to make an argument to change votin' rights. Now go get ready. We gon' take a cab down to the courthouse. It's gon' be here in an hour. I put ya' briefcase by the door so that you won't forget it."

"Thank you, Granny." She always made sure that I was prepared. I quickly showered, brushed my teeth, did my hair, and put on my new black suit. The knee-length skirt had three large pleats, and the matching jacket had three black buttons in the middle. I put on my white collared shirt, and my black patent leather shoes, finishing off my outfit with a strand of white pearls for my neck and matching pearl earrings. I grabbed my briefcase, which Granny had hung from the doorknob, and threw it over my shoulder.

Before leaving my room, I looked in my full-length mirror. There was no doubt about it—I definitely looked like a lawyer. Now, I just hoped that I would sound like a lawyer in court today. Standing there, I thought about the pictures of my mother holding what was now my briefcase. Looking at my reflection in the mirror, there was never a time that I had felt closer to her. She had always looked forward to her moment to be a lawyer, and, today, I would be living this moment for her.

I walked downstairs, where Granny and Granddaddy were waiting for me in the living room.

"There's our little esquire." Granddaddy was beaming with pride. "No matta' what happens today, Juris, we are very, very proud of you." I thanked Granddaddy, and gave him a hug. We quickly ate the breakfast that Granny had prepared, grabbed our coats, and walked outside to the cab that was waiting in front of my house.

On our ride to the courthouse, I looked at the kids on their way to school, thinking to myself, *Wow, today I could really change their rights.* I didn't want to lose this feeling of hope, as I knew that it would keep me calm as I gave my argument.

I was surprised at how relaxed I felt as I approached the courthouse, especially because the crowds of people that I saw in route to the courthouse were growing larger and larger. When we arrived at the courthouse, there was a line of people wrapped around the building. The cab driver dropped me and my family off right in front of the courthouse doors. When I walked out, the crowd started cheering, giving me another burst of confidence and assuaging all of my lingering fears.

"Juris, Juris, Juris!" I heard the crowd roar. I waved to my supporters and walked inside. After telling me goodbye, Granny and Granddaddy walked to the gallery of the courtroom, where the audience was sitting. Izzy, Maddy, Sofie, and I had planned to meet at 7:30 a.m. in front of the courtroom where I would be making the argument. I walked to the courtroom door, where Maddy was already waiting. "Isn't this cool, J.P? Today is the day that we're actually going to change the law, fingers crossed." Maddy's exuberance was contagious.

"This is awesome, Maddy!" I agreed. Sofie and Izzy strolled over to us as Maddy and I soaked in the magic of the moment.

"All of KLA is here!" Sofie announced as soon as she saw us.

"Well, guys, this is it. This is our moment. Let's go into this courtroom and change history," I said to my friends.

I grabbed my briefcase again for comfort, opened the door to the courtroom, and walked down the aisle to the lawyers' table. As I confidently strode down the courtroom aisle, with my friends walking behind me, I could feel my classmates' and teachers' eyes looking up at me. As I glanced to my left, I saw Ms. Nicholson give me a slight wave and a wink. To my right, I noticed another familiar face, but this face wasn't so comforting—it was Sly. He was wearing a sinister grin that made all of the butterflies in my stomach come rushing back.

However, I knew that I could not get unnerved; I had to keep my composure.

Finally approaching the lawyer's table, Sofie, Maddy, Izzy and I sat down. I sat at the very end of the table because I was going to be the one speaking. "Are we ready, guys?" I asked my friends, seeking their encouragement after we all sat down. I knew that the judge would be coming into the courtroom soon to start the hearing.

"We're ready, J.P.," Sofie responded. "Most importantly—you're ready. You've never been more ready." As Sofie finished her sentence, I saw the doors to the back of the courtroom open.

"All rise, court is now in session," the courtroom bailiff announced. The judge, dressed in a long black robe, walked through the back door of the courtroom. We all rose as directed. She sat down, banged her gavel, and announced, "You may all be seated." My firm, the rest of the audience and I sat down sat as directed.

"Good morning. Would counsel please announce themselves?" Although this was my first time in a real courtroom, my debate team competitions were a lot like court proceedings. I knew that the judge wanted me to introduce myself.

"Good morning, Your Honor." I stood up, assuredly. "My name is Juris Providence Prudence. I'm sitting at counsel's table with the law firm of Juris P. Prudence & Associates, which is made up of Sofia Flores-Ramirez, Isabelle Carrington, and Madeline Rosenfeld." They each stood up as I called their names. "We represent children in this case, and we are seeking their right to vote."

"Thank you, Miss Prudence," the judge responded.

"Counsel for respondent, please introduce yourself." The judge was asking our opponent to introduce himself. At the table to my right, a gray haired man stood up and started speaking. "My name is Carson Cromwell. I represent respondent, and I oppose giving children the right to vote."

"Thank you, Mr. Cromwell."

"Miss Prudence, as counsel for the complainant, please begin your argument." The complainant meant that I was the person asking the judge to make a decision.

I stood up and walked over to the podium, which sat in the middle of the two lawyers' tables. "May it please the court," I began, with a phrase that many lawyers say out of courtesy to the judge. "Your Honor, I am asking that you change the law to give kids the right to vote. My argument is based on the fact that all people are created equal. This is a right guaranteed by the Fourteenth Amendment of the Constitution of the United States of America. The Constitution applies to all people—not just people over the age of eighteen years old. That means that, if adults have the right to vote, so should kids. That is the definition of equality." I paused for a few seconds looking down at my notes.

"Throughout the history of this country, pioneers such as Susan B. Anthony and Sojourner Truth have fought to guarantee the equality of all people in this country. We have the support of over 500 people in this community who all agree that kids should have the right to vote. The time is now to change the law for kids to win the right to vote." As I finished my argument, I realized that my heart was racing. I managed to make it back to my seat, welcomed by the proud looks of my friends sitting at the lawyers' table.

"Thank you, Miss Prudence. I will now hear from the respondent," the judge said, scribbling down some notes on her pad of paper.

Carson Cromwell stood up from his seat and approached the podium. "Your Honor, with all due respect, kids getting the right to vote? What a ridiculous idea. What's next? Kids running for president?" Carson laughed sarcastically. "Let's face it. Kids are not smart enough to vote. That's why they have parents to do this for them. All this talk about everyone being equal is nonsense." Carson turned to my friends and me. "Young ladies, just be patient. You'll be adults one day. Don't rush it. Until you're adults, leave voting to the grownups." As Carson sat down, heat rushed to my face.

I was ready to respond to his argument and tell the judge all of the reasons that he was wrong.

The judge took off her glasses and rubbed her eyes. I could tell that she was considering the arguments carefully. "Miss Prudence, I'd like to hear your response to Mr. Cromwell's statement that kids are not smart enough to vote."

I couldn't believe it! The judge was asking me the same question that Granddaddy had asked me when we were practicing my argument a few days ago. I looked back at Granddaddy. With a subtle grin on his face, he nodded, and I walked back up to the podium to answer the judge's question.

"Your Honor. I'm glad that you asked that question. Kids are some of the most intelligent people on this earth. It was a thirteen-year-old child who informed the world about the atrocities happening to Jewish people during World War Two. It was children who helped organize marches in Selma, Alabama, to help African-Americans get equal voting rights in the sixties. To say that children are not smart enough to choose who will represent them in this city is ludicrous.

"Furthermore, Your Honor, kids are smart enough to know that they do not want a criminal representing them. Sylvester Sullivan was arrested for child kidnapping twenty years ago." The audience gasped as I approached the judge to give her a copy of Sylvester's arrest records.

"Objection, Your Honor! Relevance?!" Carson Cromwell stood up from his seat and slammed his fist on the table."

"Have a seat, Mr. Cromwell," the judge remarked. "Continue, Ms. Prudence."

"Kids should have a say in whether a child kidnapper should represent them. This court must grant kids the right to vote." I concluded my argument and walked back to my seat.

"Thank you, Miss Prudence and Mr. Cromwell." The judge looked up from her notepad.

"These are novel legal issues, and I need time to consider the arguments that the parties have made. We will take a brief recess so that I can retire to my chambers to make my decision. Court is adjourned until two o'clock. I will have my decision on this case then." The judge banged her gavel.

"All rise!" The bailiff ordered everyone in the courtroom to stand up as the judge rose from her bench and walked into her chambers, which was an office for judges.

"What do you think the judge thinks about our case?" Izzy asked.

"Let's talk about it when we get outside of the courtroom," I responded, nervous about who could overhear our conversation.

Izzy, Sofie, Maddy, and I quickly walked outside of the courtroom doors. As we walked into the hallway of the courthouse, our supporters assured us with their cheerful remarks.

"You're doing a great job, kids," Principal Marshall whispered to us as we walked by.

"I agree. You ladies have done remarkable work," Mrs. Cherry, our Assistant Principal complimented us.

"Thank you!" Sofie, Maddy, Izzy, and I replied in unison.

As we walked through the crowd, I wanted to find Granny and Granddaddy to find out what they thought about my argument in court, but I knew that I needed to have a conference with my friends first.

"So what did you guys think about the argument?" I asked my friends.

"I think you did a great job, J.P." Maddy stated. "It was very clear that the judge had read our law firm brief because she seemed to understand all of your arguments."

"Good job, team! I could not have made that argument without all of your help. I wish we didn't have to wait a whole hour until the judge came back with her decision. I'm on pins and needles!"

"We've done the hard work, J.P. Now all we can do is wait." Sofie calmly stated. I knew that I could count on Sofie to be the voice of reason.

"Let's get lunch," Izzy suggested. "There's no point in being hungry and nervous. Plus, I heard that the courthouse smoothies are the best in D.C.!"

We took Izzy's suggestion and walked to the courthouse deli to pass the time away.

*****

Two o'clock finally arrived and we had made our way back to the courtroom.

"All rise! Court is now in session." Everyone in the courtroom rose as the judge returned to her bench. She sat down and opened up a brown leather portfolio. She then pulled out several pieces of paper from the portfolio and glanced over the papers carefully.

She paused for what seemed like an eternity and continued, "I have considered the arguments of both of the parties. This is not an easy decision for me to make. On the one hand, we have years of law saying that a person must be eighteen years old in order to vote. On the other hand, we have very compelling arguments that were presented by Miss Prudence about why kids should have the right to vote.

"Mr. Cromwell has called the right to vote for kids 'ridiculous.' The thought of a child casting a vote might seem 'ridiculous' initially, but historical changes always seem a little out of the ordinary at first. However, years later, society looks back on the idea that may have seemed crazy several years ago, and thinks, 'How ridiculous were we not to make this change earlier?'

"Accordingly, I agree with Miss Prudence that the Fourteenth Amendment of our country's

Constitution guarantees that all persons are created equal. Kids are 'people' under the Constitution, and therefore must be treated equally. I grant kids the right to vote." The judge banged her gavel, and the courtroom exploded in cheers. Sofie, Maddy, Izzy and I started jumping up and down and finally embraced in a group hug.

Carson Cromwell walked over to my friends and me. "Well done, Miss Prudence. Congratulations." I shook his hand and thanked him. I noticed our KLA classmate, Julian Cromwell, standing beside him, wearing a sinister grin.

"Congrats, Juris. Not too many people beat my dad in court," Julian announced snidely.

"Thank you, Julian. As the judge showed us today, there's a first time for everything," I responded proudly and then turned towards Sofie, Maddy, and Izzy, who were waiting for me to join them.

My friends and I headed down the aisle where we were greeted with handshakes, claps, and pats on the back. The sounds of applause did not stop. We walked out of the courthouse doors to find the streets were filled with supporters shouting, "J.P. & Associates!" We stood on the courthouse steps, waving to our supporters and thanking them for their support.

The crowds of people slowly disappeared, and my friends and I were left standing on the steps, overwhelmed by this historic day. As we were all about to depart, I noticed Ms. Nicholson approaching us.

"Hi, Ms. Nicholson!" I exclaimed. I'd never been so happy to see her.

Ms. Nicholson, who never expressed much emotion, stood in front of me with her usual stern demeanor. "Ms. Prudence, I always wondered why more students who graduated from the KLA Law Program did not start their own law firms and do great things for this community. I imagine that they all believed that they had to be older, wiser, or have more gray hairs to do something magnificent. It astounds me that even those of us as wise, and old, and gray as I, still think this way. Thank you and your friends for showing me and this community that one doesn't have to wait to be magnificent."

Ms. Nicholson walked down the courthouse steps, leaving me and the rest of our law firm to reflect upon what she had just said. Hearing her words made us realize that all of our efforts had been worth the struggle.

CHAPTER FIFTEEN

Even though kids now had the right to vote, the final goal that we had to accomplish was making sure that Sly did not get reelected. Since the judge ruled that kids had the right to vote, people from all over the community had been reminding kids from schools all across the city to go out to the voting precincts on election day to exercise their right to vote. Election day rolled around before we knew it.

Izzy, Maddy, Sofie and I decided to go to the precinct together to cast our vote for Marty Goodlittle. After all of our hard work, it would be a shame if Sly still won the election. At the voting precinct, kids of all ages were standing in line, waiting to cast their votes. When voters noticed who we were, they rushed towards us, congratulating us on the recent court ruling.

The court ruling had put the law firm of Juris P. Prudence & Associates on the map. Our law firm had been getting flooded with calls about cases since the judge had ruled that kids should have the right to vote. People from all over the country were trying to get us to take their cases. Little did we know that this campaign would make us famous.

After we left the voting precinct, we decided to go back to my house and hold a law firm meeting and then watch the election results later that night. During our meeting, we discussed future cases that we were considering taking. Maddy had set up files for all of the calls that we had been receiving. During our meeting, we all reviewed the case files, and then held a vote about the next case that we would take.

"Okay, we have a winner." Maddy had calculated the votes for the cases.

"And the winner is…" We held our breath in anticipation, waiting for her to say the name of the case.

"The Longwood case!" Maddy announced. Our first case had concluded, but our firm was far from done making some pretty big changes in our community.

****

We concluded our meeting, ate the wholesome dinner that Granny had prepared for us, and then sat in front of the television to watch the election results. The poll numbers slowly poured in; Goodlittle and Sullivan appeared to be neck and neck, having almost an equal number of votes. The newscaster then announced that the votes from children were being counted. "With the children's vote, we can now declare the winner of the D.C. mayoral election. The winner is Marty Goodlittle!"

The newscaster's announcement caused my living room to explode in shouts of excitement. All of our hard work had paid off. Kids had the right to vote, and Sylvester Sullivan had been voted out of office.

The newscaster continued, "In other breaking news, Sylvester Sullivan has been arrested for threatening the law firm of Juris P. Prudence & Associates. He is being held in the Washington, D.C. jail without bond."

"Oh my gosh. This is great." Maddy breathed a sigh of relief.

"Yea, this is great. We are safe now," Izzy agreed.

"You look concerned, J.P.," Sofie observed.

While I was relieved, I couldn't shake the feeling that this news wasn't as good as it appeared. "Yea ... great." I tried to sound happy.

"I made my gals' favorite dessert. Let's go into the kitchen and eat." Granny announced as our excitement about all of the recent news died down. As my family and friends all departed for the kitchen, the phone rang.

"I'll get it!" I yelled. I reached for the phone.

"Hello, Juris," the voice on the other end of the phone made the hairs on my arm stand up. The voice sounded familiar. "You have crossed my family for the last time. Just remember, this isn't over." The person on the other end of the phone hung up immediately.

"I know that voice," I thought to myself. The call had shaken me so much that I wasn't able to think clearly, but I knew that I recognized the caller, and I wouldn't rest until I could pinpoint exactly who he was. Our whole case for voting rights flashed back through my mind. Something told me to review the Sullivan file again. I opened up my briefcase to grab the file. The first document that I pulled out of the file was Sly's phone records that we had found in his trash.

My eyes were immediately drawn to his call with Marvin Cromwell, Sly's previous cellmate. Seeing the name, I instantaneously knew who had called me. Julian Cromwell, my classmate. I hadn't put the pieces together until now. Marvin

Cromwell was Julian's uncle. Carson Cromwell and Marvin Cromwell were brothers. The Cromwell family was connected to Sly, and they were now out to get me and my friends.

I walked into the kitchen where my friends and grandparents were laughing and eating pie. "I'm sorry to interrupt, but I need to hold an emergency firm meeting."

"But J.P, we just finished our meeting," Izzy responded, sounding annoyed.

"Team, we have work to do, and it can't wait. Let's go!" I ordered.

I knew that if there was one thing that Julian was right about, it was the fact that our fight was far from over. During our mission to get kids the right to vote, my law firm had made new friends and new enemies, but our enemies had not stopped us from changing the law this time and, as long as my name was Juris Providence Prudence, I vowed that they would never get in the way of our fight for justice.

ABOUT THE AUTHOR

J.N. Childress is an attorney who lives in Washington, D.C. She holds a bachelor's degree in African-American Studies and Government from the University of Virginia. She also holds a law degree from the University of Virginia.

J.P.'s story is inspired by Ms. Childress' childhood dreams of becoming a lawyer and using the law to help the public. In her spare time, Ms. Childress enjoys biking around Washington, D.C. in her bright pink helmet, running, reading, and thinking about J.P. & Associates' next big case. *The Briefcase of Juris P. Prudence* is Ms. Childress' first novel.

Learn more about J.P., Maddy, Sofie, and Izzy by visiting www.jurispprudence.com!*

*Children under 13 years old must obtain parental consent.

Made in the USA
San Bernardino, CA
24 September 2014